Trafficking

Bill Ward

CHAPTER ONE

Afina longed to be back in Bucharest. Just two days earlier she was living at home with her mother and life was good. Not perfect. They had a small apartment in a tower block and she had to share a bedroom with her messy teenage sister, Adriana. Her Father had left them when her mother was pregnant with Adriana. Since that day, they had never heard from him and it was her mother who had been left to bring up a small child and a baby without any support. According to her mother, he was no great loss. He had spent too much of the limited family income on drink and too much drink inevitably led to him turning violent.

Afina had thought to look for him, now she was older, but it was not out of any deep longing to know her father, it was so she could look him in the eye and tell him how despicable he was for deserting his young family. Afina loved and admired her mother. She had always provided for them and they had never gone hungry or short of clothes.

Afina had struggled to find regular work since leaving school. Her education had been blighted by too many hours in a gym, pursuing her dream of becoming a famous gymnast and following in the footsteps of her hero, Nadia Comaneci, the first gymnast to obtain the perfect ten in an Olympic competition. While friends at school studied algebra and history, she was learning handsprings and backflips.

Her dreams had come crashing down as a fifteen year old, when she tore all the ligaments in her foot. Despite the agony, it was the look of despair she had seen on the team doctor's face, which had hurt the most. Subsequent visits to specialists had only confirmed the foot would recover for a normal life but would never again be able to take the stress required to be a world class gymnast. She had combined hard work with natural talent but in the end been defeated by bad luck

Afina's academic work continued to suffer as she struggled to adjust to a life without hope. Her gymnastics had been the way to escape the harsh reality of a poor life in Bucharest. It took her twelve months of dabbling in boys and alcohol, before she took a grip on her life and decided it was time to stop feeling sorry for herself, after one of her good friends died of a drug overdose. Fortunately, she had never really been attracted to drugs, settling for the high of alcohol but as more and more of her friends started to move from drink to drugs, she knew it was time to sort out her life or risk joining her friend in the morgue.

Afina had been left with few qualifications and no possibility of going to university but she knew she had something special, a winner's attitude. She understood what it meant to work hard, to get up early every day before school and spend two hours training and then after school going straight to the gym for a further three hours of intense training. While the hope of the Olympics burned inside her, she had been completely dedicated to her sport but when that flame was extinguished, she had temporarily lost her true self and quickly gone from winner to loser.

She had regrets, especially as no qualifications made finding work difficult, which in turn meant there was little money for going out and having fun but that was all about to end. She had been found a job working in a bar in England, by a friend of a friend, and would soon be earning enough money to live well and help her family.

More importantly, at twenty two she wanted her independence. She loved her family but she needed her own room, the freedom to wear what she wanted without comment from her mother and the option to stay out all night if she wanted. She could never invite a boy back to her apartment. Unfortunately, her mother judged all men by her father's standards, which to her mind meant they were all useless and only after one thing. Afina quite liked that one thing and didn't share her mother's opinions but if she stayed out late, it always resulted in an argument when she came home.

Her mother was worried for her daughter and had been in tears when they kissed goodbye at the airport. Afina had promised she would return home for Christmas and they could speak everyday on the phone. Afina was also nervous but it was caused by excitement not fear. She had never flown before and never left Romania. She was embarking on the first great adventure of her young life and could not wait for it to start. She would make her mother proud and start to repay her for the love and support she had always received, as she was growing up.

Afina had studied English in school and from a young age it had been her dream to visit England. Of course, she had envisaged seeing the world through gymnastics competitions but despite that never happening, the desire to travel remained. The flight took only three hours and she was met at Gatwick airport by a taxi and driven to Brighton by someone from

Timisoara, who had been living in England for three years and said it was indeed a great country, he was never going back home. She was more sure than ever she had definitely made the right decision.

She had been improving her English and reading everything about England. She knew the weather was quite different from home and wasn't surprised when she emerged from the airport to find grey skies, despite it being mid-June and having left a heatwave back home. She had pale skin and would not miss the sun too much. She was in England to make money and to properly start her adult life.

From the taxi window she had her first view of Brighton. The streets were overflowing with people and the famous pier, about which she had read so much, jutted out into the sea. It was only the third time she had ever seen the sea. The previous two times were holidays to Mamaia on the Black Sea with her last boyfriend. Brighton looked very different. For a start it had a beach of pebbles not sand, which she found very odd. Surely it was uncomfortable to sit on stones? She had a fleeting view of the pebble beach and it was surprisingly full of people, despite the lack of sunshine.

Afina had a guide book in her suitcase and there were many interesting places to visit around Brighton, which was going to keep her busy on her days off. Even London was only one hour away on the train. She was going to visit Buckingham Palace and Big Ben. She felt a sense of freedom like nothing she had ever experienced before. She could go where she wanted, when she wanted. She had made the right decision to come to Brighton.

Then the taxi had dropped her at this apartment and she had met for the first time, the man in the next room who introduced himself as Stefan. He was a tall man with a couple of days stubble on his face and unkempt hair tied back in a ponytail. He was wearing jeans and a check shirt open almost to the navel, revealing a hairy chest, which Afina didn't find very attractive. A heavy gold chain hung around his neck. The temperature in the apartment was stifling hot, which probably explained Stefan's need to undo his shirt. Perhaps in England it was normal for people to keep their homes so hot because it was always cold outside.

Almost immediately, Stefan dropped the bombshell the job was no longer available. The bar had hired someone else. He explained she had to pay him back for her flight and accommodation. She planned to do just that once she started working but now she had no job. He seemed a reasonable man and said they would be able to sort it out, she wasn't to worry. To start with she could cook and tidy for him. He would help her find other work.

She was a little concerned when he insisted on keeping her passport as otherwise she might just run off and he would be out of pocket but he had a point. He had spent a lot of money on her and it wasn't an unreasonable request so she handed it over. Anyway, she wasn't going to be needing her passport for several months, certainly not before Christmas, which was six months away.

She had tried to call home but her phone did not work, which Stefan explained was normal, it would only work within Romania. He would get her a new phone in a few days, one that worked in England. So instead, she went online and sent a message to her sister to say she had arrived safely and everything was good. She didn't mention the problem with the job as she didn't want to worry her mother. She couldn't message her mother directly because she didn't have a computer.

Afina thought her room was pleasant enough. She had a double bed and a television. There was a large mirror on one wall and a wardrobe for her clothes. It was very spacious compared with her bedroom back home but it was sterile, it lacked warmth or colour. She unpacked the picture of her family and put it beside her bed. If she ended up staying in this room very long she would buy some posters for the walls, like she had in her bedroom at home.

At Stefan's suggestion, Afina cooked some frozen pizzas for dinner and he offered her some red wine, which she didn't normally drink, preferring to drink beer on an evening out, but this was a special occasion so she had a couple of glasses. She had always helped her mother with chores and the cooking so felt well prepared to cook and clean a little for Stefan, until she found her new job.

After clearing up she returned to her room to watch television and finish unpacking. A short time later, Stefan entered her room without knocking. She looked up in surprise. She had noticed there was no lock on the inside of her door but neither did she have a lock on her bedroom at home. Perhaps Stefan was not used to having anyone stay in this bedroom so a lock had never previously been necessary.

"Would you like some more wine?" he asked.

"No, thank you," she answered in English. He had insisted she must only speak English as she needed to practise.

"Did you tell your family everything is good?"

"Yes, thanks."

He sipped at his wine and his eyes lingered over her body. She recognised the look. Her tall slim body had always attracted plenty of looks, especially after giving up gymnastics, which allowed her to eat more and in turn her body became a little more rounded and feminine. There had been two proper boyfriends in her twenty two years and quite a few other brief flings with boys. She wasn't naive. She understood men liked to look.

"Take off your clothes," Stefan instructed in a pleasant voice.

"Sorry?" She wondered if she had understood him properly.

"Take off your clothes," he commanded much less pleasantly. "I want to look at you."

Afina moved away from him until her back was against the wall. She was scared and feeling very vulnerable.

"I'm not going to wait for ever," he continued. "Take your clothes off or I'll take them off."

"I don't want to. Please don't make me," she pleaded in her native Romanian.

"Haven't I been nice to you?" he asked in English. "Haven't I spent my money on you? Provided you somewhere to live."

Afina didn't answer. She wondered if she screamed would anyone come to her aid. Stefan dwarfed her tiny frame. She was quite sure he could force her to do anything he wanted. She needed to get away but he was blocking the door, leaving no possibility of escape. She was trapped and for the first time she wondered if there had ever been a job? Had she been very foolish coming to England?

Afina made a decision. Her best chance of getting away was to pretend she liked him. Then he would relax and she would be able to escape. It was distasteful but she had no real choice. She would sneak away in the night when he was asleep. The alternative was almost certainly that he would hurt her and the end result would still be the same.

"I'm sorry, I should say thank you properly," she apologised, returning to English. "I am grateful. I am just surprised that a man such as you would like me."

Stefan smiled and relaxed. "Good. I like you very much. Now take your clothes off. Let me look at you."

She was wearing a tee shirt over jeans. She pulled the tee shirt over her head. Her breasts were small but her flat stomach and long legs gave her a model like appearance. Her face was often described as cute, occasioned by the freckles around the bridge of her nose and green eyes. Her straight, brown hair reached halfway down her back. She saw him run his tongue over his lips. She knew he approved of what he saw. She reached behind her back and undid the clasp of her bra. She was never shy in front of boys. She was proud of how she looked and knew men found her attractive. She let him feast his eyes on her breasts for a time before slowly removing her jeans.

There was a knock on the door to the apartment. Her heart jumped with joy. Maybe it was someone who could help her escape.

"Wait a minute," Stefan instructed as he moved towards the door. He seemed unconcerned by the interruption.

Afina watched as Stefan opened the door and immediately turned back towards her.

"You're late," he said, over his shoulder.

A stranger entered the room and followed him. "Damned traffic," he responded. He was shorter than Stefan but broader. He had pitch black hair, which was receding at the front, bushy dark eyebrows, matching moustache and a full beard.

The stranger noticed the half-naked Afina for the first time. "Wow, is she the new girl? Very nice."

Afina picked up her tee-shirt from the floor to cover her breasts.

"This is my friend," Stefan said. "He is going to join us. You will like him. He has a very big cock."

Afina instinctively bolted for the door. Stefan caught her around the waist and threw her back on the bed like she weighed nothing.

"We need to try you out," Stefan explained. "See if you have any talent for your new career."

"Fuck you," Afina swore.

"Exactly," Stefan laughed. "You are going to fuck us."

"She is an ungrateful little bitch," the stranger commented. "We need to teach her a lesson."

As they advanced towards her, Afina curled into a ball on the bed and begged them to leave her alone.

CHAPTER TWO

Afina could hear him moving about in the other room. She had cried herself to sleep and didn't want to get out of bed and face the monster, which was how she now viewed Stefan. He and his friend Dimitry had used her in every way imaginable before telling her to get some sleep, as she would be busy the next day. She had no doubt how they intended to keep her busy.

Dimitry had been particularly cruel. He had the largest cock she had ever known and he seemed to want to use it as a weapon to assault her mouth and anus. He didn't want to make love like her boyfriends. He had wanted to hurt her and laughed at her pain and suffering. Stefan had told him to slow down and made sure he used lube before the anal sex, saying she was too valuable to damage. She had felt like a piece of meat listening to them talk about her. It was fortunate she was on the pill because they hadn't bothered to use condoms. She hoped they didn't have any diseases.

She was sore and needed the bathroom but couldn't face getting out of bed and seeing Stefan. She needed to get away from this hell urgently. Surely he would leave the apartment at some point and then she would make her escape. She needed to be patient and gain his trust. There was nothing to be gained by a frontal assault. She needed to be cunning and take her chance when it came.

She could not just stay in bed and hope her troubles would go away. That was childish and she was not a child. When she fell trying a double somersault, she got straight back up and tried again. She fell many times but her coach always said, a winner never quits. Neither was she willing to be a victim and just another crime statistic. These animals may have taken her body but they would not take her spirit. She would make them pay for what they had done.

She was naked under the covers. She went to the wardrobe and took out the pyjamas she had never had the chance to wear the previous evening.

She opened the door to the bedroom and found Stefan sitting at the table drinking coffee.

"Morning," Stefan said, as if nothing special had occurred the previous night.

"I need the bathroom," Afina responded.

"Have some coffee first," Stefan said, indicating for her to sit down. "We need to go over the basics of living here."

She accepted the cup of coffee he poured and added a small amount of milk.

"Last night was fun," Stefan continued. "You are a beautiful girl and I have many friends who will happily pay good money for your services." Then he quickly added, "They are not all like Dimitry."

"I am not a whore."

"Neither are you an innocent virgin. It is a simple matter to have sex with men. Give them what they want and they pay well. Do this right and I will look after you."

"Last night wasn't so bad," she lied. "Sex with you was good. I just don't like Dimitry."

"Be good, make the customers happy and I promise you will not have to suffer Dimitry's huge cock again. I am sorry it was necessary but after Dimitry anyone else will seem easier." He gave an encouraging smile.

"I prefer your cock," Afina smiled rather timidly. She was determined to gain Stefan's trust. He thought she was a stupid girl. Well she wasn't and she would be the one laughing in the end.

"More coffee?" Stefan asked.

"No thanks, I need a shower," she answered. "I smell of sex." She downed the rest of her coffee and stood up.

"Help yourself. Please just remember one thing. This is my business and I take it very seriously. Do not fail me or I will give you to Dimitry and he will not be so gentle with you next time. He likes to hurt girls."

Afina had no trouble believing Dimitry would indeed enjoy hurting her if given the chance. She was sure it was only the presence of Stefan that had stopped him going further last night. She hated Stefan with a passion but by comparison with Dimitry, he seemed a saint.

She swung her hips as she walked to the bathroom, certain Stefan would be looking at her. When she locked the door behind her, she sat on the toilet and put her head in her hands. How had she been so stupid to end up in this situation? She needed not only to escape for herself but to stop any other girls back home falling into the same trap.

She tried to recall who at home had got her into this mess. Her friend knew a boy she had met in a club, who had a friend who found jobs in England. She had met someone called Dorin and it took only ten days to make the arrangements. She needed to warn her friends about Dorin. It had all been too easy to organise and that was the clue, nothing worthwhile in life ever came so easy. She should have asked more questions and made more checks. Any checks would have been a good idea! She had acted like a complete fool because of her desperation to come to England.

When she emerged from the bathroom she felt refreshed.

Stefan was on his computer. "Put on a nice dress," he instructed. "You have your first customer coming in an hour."

Afina was shocked by the revelation she had only an hour before she was expected to have sex with a complete stranger. She had thought it would only be at night she was expected to be Stefan's whore. She had hoped to sneak away during the day before any further demands were made of her body.

She said nothing but retreated to her room. She checked her watch and was surprised to find it was already eleven. She had slept late and her appointment was probably for midday. She realised there could be no escape in the next hour. What would this stranger expect of her? What would he look like? She needed to prepare but what should she wear? Too many unnecessary questions, she was driving herself mad. She needed to get a grip.

Afina decided to wear a simple black dress as it would be easier to remove than jeans. Her white underwear was new and surely any man would find her attractive with her dress removed. She spent some time brushing her hair and doing her makeup. She looked at herself in the mirror. He would not be disappointed with how she looked. She had to focus on doing everything to make Stefan happy so she could escape. She would think about that while she let this stranger fuck her.

Afina returned to the living room where Stefan was still staring at his computer. "I'm hungry. Can I make something to eat?" she asked.

"You look great," Stefan said, looking up from his computer. "There's some eggs in the fridge and bread on the side. Make us some eggs on toast."

Afina made the food and some fresh coffee. As they sat to eat, Stefan's phone rang. He answered and she understood by Stefan's replies that the caller was asking about her availability. She heard Stefan say that she provided all services, which made her almost choke on her breakfast.

"You are going to be very popular," Stefan said, as he put his phone down on the table and resumed eating. "You will soon pay off what you owe me and be making good money for yourself."

"What am I expected to do for these men?" Afina asked, working hard to control the anger and revulsion she was feeling.

"You give them sex and a blowjob. For sex they must wear a condom. They pay for your time. The minimum is thirty minutes. Most men stay an hour. If they want anal sex they must pay extra but I will tell you if they have paid for extras."

Afina was wondering if Stefan thought she was a complete idiot or did she have slut written on her forehead in large letters? Did he really expect her to just accept becoming his whore? From what Dimitry had said, it was obvious there had been other girls before her. What had happened to them? Had they been allowed to leave once their debt was repaid? She was left with an uneasy feeling.

Afina glanced around the apartment looking for evidence of other girls but could see nothing. Her eyes settled on the door leading to freedom. She had already come to the conclusion that the layout of the apartment made escape extremely difficult. The outside door from the hallway led into the living space of kitchen and lounge. There were two bedrooms and a bathroom which all led from the living space. The apartment was on the third floor so jumping from a window wasn't an option. The only escape was through the front door but that required getting past Stefan.

She had asked about food, planning to offer to go shopping and then disappear but Stefan had explained the supermarket delivered a standard order every Friday so that was another dead avenue. She had asked him to add a few things she liked to the shopping list, which she hoped would make him think she had accepted she would not be leaving.

She thought her best chance of escape would be at night when Stefan was asleep in the other bedroom, which meant she had to be strong and get through the day. She carried the plates to the sink and then went to her room to prepare for her visitor. She once again had started to wonder what he would be like. Hopefully nothing like Dimitry. Was it possible he might even help her if she told him of her plight? She decided that would be a bad idea. He might indeed be a friend of Stefan and this could be a further test.

Her mind turned to what he would expect sexually. She hoped he wouldn't want anal sex. Despite having enjoyed it in the past, after her experience with Dimitry, she didn't fancy having it again so quickly.

She heard a knock at the door and Stefan greeting someone. She had intentionally left her bedroom door ajar so she could hear what was said.

"How long do you want to stay?" Stefan asked. "Prices start at sixty pounds for half an hour and it's one hundred pounds for an hour."

"An hour please," came the response in a mature English voice without accent.

It was an Englishman, Afina was quite certain. She wasn't entirely sure why but she was pleased he wasn't Romanian. She had never had an Englishman before. In fact, she had only ever had sex with Romanians. At school she had learned about English gentlemen. They were polite and wouldn't behave like Dimitry.

"Afina, come out here, please. You have a visitor," Stefan called out pleasantly.

As Afina walked into the lounge she saw the stranger for the first time. He was older than she had expected. In fact he was old enough to be her father. He was dressed very smartly in a striped, blue suit and looked like a businessman. His hair was short and grey. She relaxed a little. He did not look like a man who would want to hurt her.

He turned towards her and a large smile crossed his face.

"Hello," she said. "I am Afina."

"You're gorgeous," the man replied.

"Thank you."

"An hour," Stefan said simply.

Afina led him back to her room and closed the door.

CHAPTER THREE

Afina lay on her bed thinking about the last few hours. It was four in the afternoon. Sex with the businessman had been easier than she had anticipated. He had been very undemanding and allowed her to take charge. At first she had tried to block her mind to feeling anything but the familiar sensations had stirred a little when he went down on her and though it was not great sex, it had not been entirely unpleasant.

Although the man had paid for one hour, the sex only lasted half the time and then he had sat beside her on the bed and talked about his work and his family. She was tempted to ask for his help but thought it too risky. He almost certainly would be married and wouldn't want to get involved with the police and risk having his secret visit to a whore discovered, so she said nothing.

When the man left, Afina heard Stefan ask him if everything was okay and she was pleased he had answered very positively. He planned to come again soon. He won't be coming with me anytime soon, she smiled to herself. I'm out of here tonight.

Stefan had informed her there was another customer for her arriving in ten minutes. She had showered and was ready for him. She once again heard the knock at the door. He was ten minutes early. She was shocked when she heard a female voice coming from the next room. She had never had sex with a girl.

"Afina, come out here," Stefan called out.

She walked apprehensively into the lounge.

"This is Mara," Stefan introduced the new girl. "She will be working with you. The next customer always has two girls."

Mara was wearing just red underwear and with her dark tan and long black hair looked quite stunning.

"Hello," Afina said with a friendly smile. She was happy to meet another girl from back home.

"New girl?" Mara asked, turning to Stefan and ignoring Afina.

"Very new but she shows promise."

"Just do whatever I tell you," Mara said in an unfriendly voice.

Afina was shocked by Mara's cold attitude. She wondered what the relationship was between her and Stefan. She didn't have long to dwell on the thought as there was a further knock at the door.

Stefan opened the door and a large, muscular man entered. He looked mid-thirties and was wearing smart designer clothes. There was a strange jagged scar on his thick neck. He had an air of importance. Certainly Stefan seemed extra respectful in his welcome.

"Good to see you again, Victor," Stefan said, shaking his hand.

"And you, Stefan." He turned towards Mara and gave her a kiss on each cheek. "Hello, Mara." Then he stood in front of Afina and looked her up and down. "So this is the new girl. She looks good."

Afina could immediately detect the Romanian accent.

"Her name's Afina," Stefan replied. "She is very good."

Victor was staring Afina in the eyes. "So are you good?" he asked after a moment.

"You can decide after I fuck you," Afina said quietly but clearly, returning his stare.

"I think I am going to like this one," Victor said, turning towards Stefan. "She has spirit. I like spirit in a girl. It makes for an interesting challenge to tame such a girl."

"Afina, why don't you take Victor to your room? I will join you in a minute." Mara suggested.

Afina led the way to her room, thinking she was no bloody wild animal that needed taming, even though she was now living in what seemed like a cage. Once in the room she turned to face Victor. She pulled her dress up over her body to reveal lacy, matching white underwear, she had purchased especially for her trip to England.

"Very nice," Victor said admiringly.

Mara entered carrying something under her arm. Afina's view of exactly what she placed on the floor was obstructed by Victor.

"Shall we start?" Victor asked.

"Afina, take off your underwear and lie on your stomach on the bed," Mara commanded.

Afina did as instructed. Victor removed his clothes and climbed on the bed, kneeling on either side of Afina's back, pinning her to the bed. He massaged her shoulders a little then took both her hands in his.

Afina noticed a naked Mara at the side of the bed and then felt her clamp the handcuffs around her wrist. Mara stretched her hand towards the corner of the bed and she felt the handcuffs being attached to a metal ring bolted into the corner of the bed, which she hadn't previously noted. Afina was nervous but could do nothing with Victor's weight on her back. Next, Mara handcuffed her other hand to the other corner of the bed. At the same time she felt Victor kissing her neck and relaxed a little.

Afina felt a loop encircling each ankle and both of her legs were secured so she was spread-eagled on the bed. The position was mildly uncomfortable but she was more concerned by her vulnerability than her physical discomfort.

Victor placed the only chair in the room next to the bed, close to Afina's face and sat down. She looked at him uncertain what was going to happen next. She had her first view of his cock and she was pleased to see he certainly was no Dimitry.

Victor gently stroked her cheek. "Mara is going to beat you now," he said in a soothing voice. "After each stroke I want you to count the strokes."

It took a second for what he had said to sink in and then Afina desperately tried to free her arms and legs but she was securely held. The stinging pain from a cane on her bottom made her body jerk off the bed. "Stop," she screamed. "Please don't."

"This is your last warning," Victor warned. "Count the strokes. If you don't do this properly we will start your twenty strokes again until you get it right."

Afina felt the pain of another stroke on her bottom. "Why are you doing this to me," she screamed. "Let me out of here."

"Behave yourself and count the strokes," Victor said sharply. "We will begin again."

Afina realised she was only making matters worse by not doing as instructed. She counted out loud after each of the strokes. For seven strokes she was silent but then the pain became too much to bear. She screamed out in pain after each blow before counting the number out loud.

After twenty strokes, she prayed he would not change his mind and there would be no further pain. Tears streamed down her cheeks and she was whimpering.

"Well done," Victor said. "That is enough for today. Now I would like to cum."

She noticed his average sized cock was now standing rigid, excited by what he had seen. He placed it against her lips and she obediently opened her mouth to allow him inside. She lay with her head sideways on the pillow while he thrust into her mouth. In just a couple of minutes he grunted and she felt him explode in her mouth.

"Swallow everything," he commanded.

Afina did as she was told. She was too scared of him to resist. She just wanted this ordeal to be over.

"Thank you, Afina. I look forward to seeing you again soon," Victor said, reaching for his clothes. "You show great promise. We will soon have you taking fifty strokes."

Afina was feeling very weak, almost faint. She felt Victor kiss her on the cheek and then heard the door to the bedroom opening and closing.

Her legs were freed and then her arms.

"Don't move, I have some cream to put on your bottom. It will help with the pain," Mara said kindly.

Afina was too shocked to move. She felt the cream being applied and it did soothe her skin.

"Take these," Mara said, offering three pills. "They will also help with the pain."

Afina was recovering her strength. She sat up and swallowed the pills with a swig from a bottle of water, Mara offered.

"How could you do that to me?" Afina asked.

"I'm sorry but if I don't do it one of the men will and they are a lot harder."

"Why didn't you warn me what you were going to do?"

"There is simply no way of preparing you for that. It's best this way. Otherwise you would have refused and fought us and then Victor would have given you thirty strokes or more even."

Afina was surprised by the change in Mara. She was no longer cold and unfriendly.

"I can't stay here," Afina announced. "Help me escape. I don't belong here."

"I can't."

"Please," Afina begged.

"You mustn't try and run away," Mara cautioned. "They will catch you and make you regret the day you were born. I have seen these men take a knife to a girl." She shuddered at the memory.

"Why are you different?" Afina asked. "You are free to come and go. You get to beat me not be beaten. Why?"

"I am useful to him."

"Are you his girlfriend?"

"Stefan doesn't have girlfriends. Not in the way you mean. He just has women he fucks when he feels like it."

"How are you useful to him?" Afina asked.

"That is not your business," Mara snapped. "You ask too many questions."

"I am not staying here," Afina said with conviction. "I would rather die than live this life."

"And you will wish you are dead if they catch you trying to escape. You don't want to give Victor or Dimitry an excuse to enjoy themselves. Let me warn you also that Stefan locks the downstairs door every night before going to bed. Only he has the key so there is no escape."

"Where do you live?" Afina asked.

"Downstairs."

"Downstairs?" Afina queried.

"Yes. Stefan owns the whole building. He and Dimitry have a number of girls living in the different apartments. I live one floor down."

Afina was disappointed to hear everyone in the building worked for Stefan. It would make escape harder.

"Stefan obviously thinks you're special," Mara said. "Only the special girls get to stay in his apartment. He must have big plans for you."

"What do you mean?"

"I've said enough. You should go take a shower and clean up. I need to get back downstairs."

Mara moved towards the door. "I'll see you around," she said and then was gone.

Afina waited a few minutes, thinking about the last forty eight hours. It was difficult to believe how her life had changed in such a short time. She knew with absolute certainty she was prepared to do anything to escape. She would even be prepared to kill Stefan if necessary. Of course, that was easier said than done.

She took a look at her rear in the mirror and was shocked by what she saw. There were large raw looking welts covering her bottom. She was going to be black and blue tomorrow and sitting was going to be uncomfortable. Mara had beaten her hard but she was correct when she said a beating from a man would be far worse. Maybe Mara wasn't such a bitch after all. Anyway, Afina doubted Mara had much choice in delivering the beating. Afina couldn't imagine any girl saying no to the likes of Stefan or Victor when they demanded something.

She needed a shower or perhaps for a change she would soak in a bath. Most importantly, she needed to brush her teeth and get the stench of Victor out of her mouth.

Stefan was again at his computer when she entered the lounge.

"Mara said you did good," Stefan said. "Victor only visits us a couple of times a month and he likes a variety of girls."

Afina ignored him and went straight to the bathroom. She locked the door and started to run a bath. She went to the widow and looked out. It wasn't ideal but this was going to have to be her escape route.

CHAPTER FOUR

Afina had heard no sounds for the last couple of hours. Stefan had gone to bed at midnight and it was time to make her move. She quietly slipped out from under the duvet. She was dressed in jeans, jumper and trainers. All her other clothes she would be leaving behind as she couldn't carry a suitcase through the window.

She was feeling both nervous and excited. Feelings she had regularly experienced before competitions. Some competitors would throw up before they went out to compete but she managed to control her nerves. Mara's warnings about what they would do to her if they caught her, meant she was entirely focused on what lay ahead. Prior to a competition, the coach would talk to them about the need to 'be in the zone.' That had never been more true than now, when she considered her life to be in danger if she was caught.

She tiptoed to the door and listened again for any sound of danger. Hearing nothing, she opened the door and then slowly moved across the lounge floor. Her eyes were fixed on the door to Stefan's room as she made her way to the bathroom. If there was any noise now, she was still relatively safe. She would simply call out that she needed to pee although if he saw how she was dressed she would be in trouble.

The house was old and a floorboard squeaked, causing her to stand perfectly still and listen for any reaction from Stefan's room. Nothing disturbed the silence so she continued to the bathroom. As she locked the door behind her, she felt a sense of relief and breathed out for the first time since leaving her bedroom. So far so good.

Afina opened the window and peered out into the darkness. There was just enough moonlight to see the ground below. She knew the climb down would be dangerous in daytime let alone the semi darkness but she had no choice. She simply had to get away.

She had previously identified the cast iron guttering looked quite solid and her hope was it would support her weight, at least some of the way to the ground. She knelt on the windowsill looking into the bathroom and reached for the gutter. As a young gymnast she had been able to climb ropes and was generally light on her feet. She hoped all those hours of training would finally turn out to be useful.

She wrapped her hands around the gutter and then said a small prayer as she swung her legs out into the void before gripping the gutter with her knees and ankles. The gutter creaked but held firm. It was fortunate she was so light. She slowly moved downwards. As she came parallel with a window on the second floor she smiled at her progress, knowing she was a third of the way towards safety. Even now, if she fell, she might have a chance.

She descended another ten feet and she began to relax. In just another few feet she would be safe and the moment her feet touched the ground she was going to run as fast as she could, as far away from this hell as possible.

She didn't wait to reach the ground but sprung down the last few feet. She landed lightly on her toes. It would have deserved a ten from any judge. She was in the small patio garden, which was completely overrun with weeds and bushes. She crouched down low and listened but there were no shouts from above indicating her escape had been detected.

Afina had identified the side gate as her means to exit the garden and now moved towards it, careful not to make too much noise. The gate opened easily enough and she found herself in an alley running down the side of the building. She crept in the direction of the front of the building and looked out onto a quiet road. The road was well lit, which made her nervous about leaving the comfort of the shadows where she was hiding. There was no sound and no signs of life so she turned to the right and walked quickly towards safety. She didn't want to run and attract attention but after a few yards the urge was too great and she started to sprint. She had no idea where the road led but didn't care, she was free.

After a short distance, the road turned to the left and went uphill for a short time before joining a major road lined with shops. Afina stopped and drew a further deep breath. The fresh air of freedom tasted extra good. A sense of exhilaration unlike anything she had ever experienced coursed through her body.

She was surprised to find the road was quite busy even at this late hour. She glanced at her watch to check she hadn't left earlier than planned. It was three in the morning but there were cars going in both directions and a few people walking past. This wasn't like the suburb of Bucharest where she lived. At this time of night it would be deserted. She didn't have any idea which direction she should take but settled for turning right and walked at a fast pace. She was feeling more and more elated with every step she took.

She had only gone fifty yards when she saw a man walking towards her and her heart skipped a beat. There was no mistaking Dimitry's stocky build and menacing, dark looks. She saw the sudden look of recognition on his face and immediately turned in blind panic and started to run.

She had about twenty metres head start and cast a glance over her shoulder to see he was gaining.

"Help me! She screamed at the top of her voice but at no one in particular. "Please help me!"

She could hear Dimitry's footsteps pounding on the pavement, getting closer.

Afina saw the couple ahead start running in her direction. She took a second to register they were wearing uniforms. In the same instant she recognised they were almost certainly police officers, she felt the hand grab her jacket from behind and pull her to a stop.

"Let go of her," the female police officer demanded as she came close.

"Fuck off," Dimitry replied and started to pull Afina away from the officers. "She belongs to me."

"Let go of her now," the male police officer also demanded, moving to block Dimitry's path.

Dimitry threw Afina to the ground and in the same moment his right hand reached inside his belt and withdrew a six inch blade, which without warning, he stabbed into the police officer's chest.

As Afina landed on the ground she tried to squirm away from Dimitry and looked up to see him brandishing the knife in the direction of the police woman. The male police officer had fallen to his knees but suddenly reached out and wrapped his arms around Dimitry's legs, trying to pull him to the ground. The female police officer was circling Dimitry with a baton in her hand, trying to land a blow.

Afina had crawled a few feet away and climbed unsteadily to her feet. Dimitry was trying to free his legs and lunging out with his knife towards the policewoman. For a second her eyes locked with those of the young policewoman who shouted, "Run!"

In that moment, Afina saw Dimitry stab the policewoman and she fell to the ground clutching at her chest. Afina felt a sickening sense of guilt, brought on by the knowledge she had been responsible for this young girl being stabbed. She had never felt such despair. She knew the image of the poor girl's white shirt turning crimson would stay with her for the rest of her life.

She reasoned there was nothing she could do to help the police girl so turned and fled without looking back. She took the first turning off the main road and then another turning, always heading away from the devil that was Dimitry. She listened for steps running after her but there was nothing. The quiet was broken only by the sound of at least two police sirens rushing to the scene.

Adrenaline carried her a long way but she had been running uphill and eventually she had to slow to a walk. She was at a roundabout with several roads running off in different directions. She had no idea which direction to take. Turning right had been a terrible decision last time so she was thinking left must be a better bet when she saw a couple of young girls approaching. Afina was bent double, trying to catch her breath.

"You alright?" one of the girls asked. She had short blonde hair and a rather masculine appearance.

"No." Afina answered. In truth she was feeling desperate. "Someone just tried to rape me and I only just escaped."

"Oh my God! That's awful," the other girl responded. She had a number of tattoos and piercings but was still very feminine, with longer, brown hair than her friend and a fresh, pretty face. "Shall we call the police?"

"No," Afina replied hurriedly. "No police." Tears were running down her cheeks. She wiped the tears away with her sleeve. "I'm alright now, just a bit shocked by what happened."

The first girl put her arm around Afina's shoulder. "Look, we live just a minute away. Do you want to come back to our place and rest up for a bit? Then we can get you a taxi home."

Afina was overjoyed. "Thank you," she said, wiping her eyes. She could explain later she no longer had a home that could be reached by taxi. She just needed to get off the road for a bit, in case Dimitry was searching for her. "That would be very nice of you." She was already feeling safer in their company.

"I'm Emma," the blonde introduced herself. "And this is Becky."

"Thank you so much, I am Afina."

"That's a lovely name," said Emma. "Where are you from?"

"Romania."

"Right, let's go get a cup of tea or something stronger, if you prefer and then we'll sort out that taxi."

CHAPTER FIVE

No one delivers good news at four thirty in the morning. The sound of the doorbell awakened him from a deep sleep. He didn't immediately open his eyes, not sure if he had been dreaming but then the bell rang twice more in quick succession and he knew there really was someone at his front door, in the middle of the night. There was a nervous knot in his stomach as he climbed from his bed and took his dressing gown from where it hung behind the bedroom door.

As he descended the stairs, he switched on the hall lights, announcing to whoever was outside that he was awake. He glanced at the mirror on the wall and ran his hands through his hair to make himself look a little more presentable. He looked tired not just because his sleep had been disturbed. There were too many lines around his eyes and his hair was turning grey in places. Craggy faced was about the best compliment he was ever likely to receive.

He checked the chain was on the front door as he opened it a few inches. He couldn't imagine anyone intent on doing him physical harm, would be standing on the other side of the door but it was best to be cautious. He had spent twenty years being extremely cautious.

"Mr. Powell?" the man in the suit asked. Beside him stood a policeman in uniform,

"Yes."

"I'm Chief Inspector Brown. Can we come in please, Sir?"

"Is it about my daughter?" Powell asked, desperately hoping for a negative response.

"Yes, Sir. Can we speak inside please?"

Powell checked the warrant card the Chief Inspector was proffering, which seemed in order. He closed the door again so he could remove the chain and then stood back to allow the two policemen to enter. He didn't want to let them in. He wanted to go back to bed and wake up having had a bad dream. He was quite sure what he was about to experience would be his worst nightmare. If it was a trivial matter they would have spoken to him on his doorstep. Powell had studied both policemen's faces. He could see the warning signs in the Chief Inspector's discomfort. The second officer had tried to avoid Powell's gaze altogether. Coming inside could only mean bad news.

Powell's anxiety had increased a hundredfold as he led them silently through to the living room. Conversation wasn't necessary. There was no urgency to hear terrible news. He was still clinging to hope, which would inevitably disappear once the Chief Inspector revealed his reason for being present.

Powell sat on his favourite leather chair and the policemen sat themselves on the sofa.

"I'm afraid we have some bad news," the Chief Inspector began. "In the early hours of this morning, while out on patrol, your daughter and a colleague have been attacked..."

Powell knew he was now in the last chance saloon. He gripped the arms of his chair praying Bella was only injured. The Chief Inspector's next words crushed his last hope.

"I'm terribly sorry to have to inform you that your daughter died in the ambulance on the way to hospital."

"How did she die?" Powell asked in a steady voice masking his emotions. Inside his mind he was no longer sitting in his lounge. He was remembering the tiny bundle of joy born twenty years ago with a dark mop of hair. Remembering the first time he held Bella in his arms and promised to always protect her. He'd failed her as badly as he'd failed her mother.

"I'm afraid I don't yet know many details about what happened," the Chief Inspector replied.

"Where did they take her? Which hospital?"

"Sussex County."

Powell was on his feet in a second. "I need to go see her."

"Is there someone you can call, Sir? To be with you."

"I don't need anyone to hold my hand," Powell snapped. "I need to go see Bella. I'm going upstairs to get dressed and then I'm going to the hospital."

"Sir, Bella is dead," the Chief Inspector stressed.

"I heard you the first time, Chief Inspector. I simply wish to see her and say goodbye." Powell wasn't going to share the real reason for his urgency to see his daughter's body. "Now if you don't mind, I'm in a hurry." Powell used his arm to point towards the front door, indicating he wanted the policemen to leave.

Almost reluctantly the two policemen followed Powell to the front door.

"We all liked Bella," the Chief Inspector said, on the doorstep. "We are terribly sorry for your loss. I will be in touch again tomorrow when I know more of the facts."

"Thank you, Chief Inspector." Powell closed the door to end any possibility of further conversation or delay.

He retraced his steps to the bedroom where such a short time earlier he had been in a deep sleep, blissfully unaware of how his life was about to be torn apart for the second time. He was almost grateful Bella's mother was no longer alive and having to endure this pain but thinking of her only compounded his feelings of guilt. He had failed them both so terribly and there would be no second chances.

There were people to be called but they could wait. His own mother lived in the warmth of Lanzarote where she had moved five years earlier after the death of his father. Vanessa's mother similarly lived alone in Bournemouth, after her husband died of cancer just a couple of years after Vanessa was murdered. If cancer could be brought on by a broken heart then that was what had happened. Both grandmothers were going to be devastated by Bella's death.

From Powell's home in Hove it took only fifteen minutes to reach the hospital. The roads were deserted but despite the urgency, Powell kept to the speed limits. Less than an hour had passed since the knock on his door to when he was staring at Bella's lifeless body on a trolley. Her birth certificate said Isabella but she had only ever been called Bella. She had been a beautiful baby and grown into a beautiful young woman.

Powell had been given a private room to say his farewells and asked to be alone when the nurse had appeared to be planning to stay in the room. Bella looked serene and peaceful. All but her face was covered by a white sheet. He pulled the sheet back to reveal her naked body. He felt uncomfortable looking at her naked but he needed to see first-hand how she had died. There was evidence of a knife wound below her left breast. He took his phone from his pocket and took several pictures from different angles.

"I'm sorry darling," Powell spoke softly. "I swear I will find whoever is responsible for this and when I do they will wish they had never been born."

He remembered their last conversation a couple of days earlier. She had been rushing out for a late shift and they had barely spoken but he remembered her last words were, "I love you."

He was a short step from completely disintegrating and fought back the tide of dark emotion that was trying to envelop him. He needed to focus and remain strong. There would be time later for grieving.

Powell replaced the sheet. He stroked her hair, pushing it away from her face, and leaned forward to kiss her lightly on the lips. He stood up straight and gazed upon his daughter's body for the last time. Then he turned and strode purposefully out of the room.

CHAPTER SIX

Afina awoke from a nightmare infested sleep and breathed a sigh of relief when she heard Emma and Becky talking in the kitchen. It had not all been a bad dream. She had escaped from Dimity and Stefan. She was safe, at least for the time being but she had witnessed the two police officers who came to her rescue both being stabbed. She wondered if they were dead. If so, it was all her fault.

She threw back the blanket and sat up on the couch that had been her bed for the night. She glanced at her watch. It was ten thirty. She picked up her jeans from the floor and pulled them on, then headed for the sound of the voices, which were coming from the kitchen.

"Morning," Emma said, as she spotted Afina. "Would you like some tea or coffee?"

"Coffee please."

"How did you sleep?" asked Rebecca.

"Good, thank you."

Afina could not believe how lucky she had been to find these girls. They had taken her home and given her a large brandy, after which they had offered her the chance to sleep on their couch. Somehow they seemed to understand she was in trouble and hadn't bombarded her with too many questions. She didn't want to call the police and didn't want a taxi, as she had no money and nowhere to stay.

Emma filled a mug with fresh filter coffee and placed it on the small table. "Help yourself to milk and sugar," she said.

Rebecca put a plate containing toast in the middle of the table. "Help yourself," she said.

Afina sat down at the table and added a small amount of milk to her coffee. "You are both very kind," she said.

"I'm glad we were able to help," Emma answered, taking the chair opposite Afina. She shot a glance at Becky before continuing. "Becky and I have been talking and we've agreed that if you want to stay for a few days while you sort yourself out that will be fine with us."

"That's if you don't mind the couch," Becky said, smiling and sitting in the remaining chair.

"Really? You don't mind?"

"You're in a foreign country with no money and nowhere to stay. It's the least we can do," stressed Becky.

For the first time in a long while, Afina smiled broadly. "Thank you so much."

They drank coffee and ate toast with Afina answering questions about where she lived and her family. She said nothing about how she came to be in England.

Afina was intrigued by Becky, who had piercings in her tongue, nose and multiple ones in her ears. "Did your piercings hurt?" Afina asked.

"The tongue hurt like hell but it was worth it. Emma loves it."

"It has its benefits," Emma laughed.

Afina didn't understand what Emma meant about benefits. She realised her English still needed improving because when the girls spoke quickly she struggled to follow what they were saying.

"Do you like them?" Becky asked.

"They are quite nice but I wouldn't want one in my tongue. I had a boyfriend once who suggested I get one but it was only because, you know, he thought it would feel good."

"That's boys for you, always thinking about their dicks!" Becky replied.

"Dicks?" Afina asked.

"You know, their penis." Emma explained.

"Why is it called a dick? Isn't Dick a name?"

Emma and Becky looked at each other then burst into laughter.

"I have no fucking idea why it's called a dick," Emma said.

"Don't ask me," Becky said. "I haven't a clue and whatever they're called, I don't like them!"

"Becky has some other piercings in interesting places," Emma volunteered.

"Afina doesn't want to know about them," Becky quickly responded.

"They must have hurt," Afina stated firmly.

"Being serious for a moment," Emma said. "What else can we do to help you, Afina?"

"The first thing I must do is to call my family in Romania and let them know what has happened."

"There's a phone in the lounge," Emma said. "Go call them."

"Really? You don't mind?"

"Well don't spend hours talking to them but otherwise it's fine," Emma smiled.

"Thank you so much. I don't know how I will ever repay you for your kindness."

"Us girls have to stick together," Becky chipped in.

Afina hurried to the lounge and dialled the number for home.

"It's me, mama," she said excitedly, on hearing the familiar voice answer.

"Afina, where are you? What's happened? Why didn't you call me?" her mother responded anxiously. "There was a man here earlier asking if we had heard from you. I thought something had happened to you. Why was he visiting me before breakfast. I wasn't even dressed. This man would not leave his name but he said to tell you to contact Stefan urgently. Who is Stefan?"

Afina was temporarily lost for words. "Just a friend," she answered after a moment. Who was this man who had visited her family? Was it a threat? Was he letting her know they could find her family and hurt them if they wanted?

"Afina, are you in trouble? I didn't like this man."

"No, everything is okay, mama," she lied. She wasn't sure what to say but didn't want to frighten her mother. "But mama, I had my bag stolen so I have no money or passport."

"Perhaps Stefan has found it and wants to return it. That's why he wants you to contact him urgently."

"No mama, Stefan doesn't have it," Afina answered and then recognised it would have been easier to simply agree with her mother.

"Have you reported it to the police?"

"Yes mama but you know what it's like. Bags are stolen all the time and there is no chance of it being found so I have no money. Can you please send me some?"

"Of course, my love. How do I do it?"

Afina realised she didn't know how to transfer money abroad. She knew it was possible but how? She would ask her new friends.

"Mama, I will check the best way and call you back later. Thank you, mama. I will pay you back when I get a job."

"Don't you have a job, Afina? I thought you were working in a bar."

"They didn't need me at the bar so I must find another job. Don't worry, mama. There are plenty of jobs here in England."

"Come home, Afina."

"I can't mama. I don't have a passport."

"Go to the embassy. They will give you a new passport."

"I will mama but that takes time and I will have to go to London."

"Remember this is your home, Afina. Come back soon."

"I need to go now mama and talk to my friends and ask them what is the best way to transfer money. I will call you back later."

"Love you."

"And you, mama."

Afina ended the call in shock. Stefan knew where she lived and she could not go home. She didn't know what to do. She returned to the kitchen.

"Everything okay?" Emma asked.

"Yes," Afina responded with a half-hearted smile. "What is the best way for my mother to send me some money?"

"I'm not sure but Becky can get you some more coffee while I check on the internet."

"Thank you."

"And don't worry about some cash for the next day or two," Emma continued. "I can lend you some money to tide you over."

Afina couldn't help herself. She burst into tears. "I don't know what I would have done without you both," she said, wiping the tears from her eyes.

"As Becky said, us girls have to stick together."

CHAPTER SEVEN

Powell opened the door to the Chief Inspector and again showed him through to the lounge. This time he came alone, no longer needing the prop of another officer, with no terrible news to deliver. Thirty six hours had passed since his last visit, some of the worst hours of Powell's life. He had resorted to whisky to try and numb the pain but it hadn't helped, just made him even more morose. Powell offered tea, which was declined and then they occupied the same seats as before.

"So, Chief Inspector what more can you tell me about Bella's death?"

"I'm afraid, as we have an ongoing investigation, there is little detail I can provide. Bella was on patrol with Constable Myers when they stumbled upon an argument between a man and a woman. They tried to intervene but the man stabbed both of them."

"So you have this man in custody?"

"No we don't. We have the incident captured on CCTV, which is how we know what happened. Constable Myers is still in Intensive Care and we haven't been able to interview him."

"Where did this happen?"

"Western Road."

"And the woman?"

"She ran from the scene and that really is as much as I can tell you."

"Have you been able to identify the man or woman?" Powell persisted.

"Not yet but we will," the Chief Inspector stated with conviction. "At least we know what they both look like. I will keep you informed of progress," he said, rising from his chair.

"So this looks like a case of a simple domestic gone badly wrong?" Powell asked, ignoring the Chief Inspector's attempt to end the questioning and staying seated.

"I'm sorry Mr. Powell…"

"Please, everyone just calls me Powell."

"Powell, I really can't answer any more questions. Please be assured we are doing everything possible to locate the man who murdered your daughter. She was one of us and though she was quite new, she was very popular. Every single Officer is in off leave, going door to door with a photo of this man. We will find him."

Powell realised he wasn't going to get any further information so shook hands and escorted the Chief Inspector to the door. At least they were keeping him informed and getting visits from a Chief Inspector probably wasn't the norm but reflected Bella's death was being given the highest possible attention. Not that Powell believed one death was any more important than any other, except to those immediately affected by the loss of someone they loved.

He returned to the lounge deep in thought. It appeared his Bella had simply been in the wrong place at the wrong time. He had no doubt the police would do everything in their powers to bring Bella's killer to justice. They looked after their own but he could not sit around and do nothing. He would also start looking for this man, he shouldn't be too hard to locate.

Powell decided he needed more information. He couldn't rely on just what he was being drip fed by the local police. He didn't want to make the call but there really was no other way. It had been almost twenty years since he last spoke to anyone. Twenty years since Vanessa was killed and he almost lost Bella. Now she was gone too. It was Bella who had pulled him through those difficult early years. Young children didn't allow you to sit around feeling sorry for yourself. But at night the demons had come and the nightmares which reminded him of how he failed Vanessa. The passing of time made it easier but he had never forgotten and the guilt had never fully gone away.

So he dialled the number that was only meant for an absolute emergency even though this wasn't the type of emergency envisaged when he was given the number. He wasn't sure if the number would even still be valid after so many years. After a short time, a female voice answered. He gave his code number and explained he needed to speak with Brian Cooper, not knowing for certain he would still be alive, let alone doing the same job. He was put on hold and then a male voice came on the line.

"This is the duty officer," the man stated. "How can I help you?"

"I wish to speak with Brian Cooper," Powell reiterated.

"Mister Cooper is a very busy man. I'm sure I can help you."

"Please tell him to call Powell. It's urgent."

"Look Powell, someone of his seniority isn't just going to call back every Tom, Dick and Harry, without a damn good reason. What is this about?"

"Just as well then my name's Powell, not Tom or Dick or Harry," he replied sarcastically. He was just about keeping his anger in check. "Tell him it's about Bella. I guarantee you he will want to call me." Powell ended the call to save further discussion.

So Brian was not only alive but someone in a senior position. Powell wasn't surprised to hear his old friend's career had progressed positively and was pleased by the news, as it would make it easier for him to provide help.

CHAPTER EIGHT

Afina had realised as the day went on that Emma and Rebecca were more than just friends. They held hands and kissed like any lovers. She had also been invited in their bedroom to find a change of clothes and there was just the one large double bed. Afina had been careful to hide her bottom when she tried on the clothes. It had turned a bright blue and yellow colour and wasn't something she wanted to have to explain.

Afina had no problem with her new friends being lovers. She had never previously known any other lesbians and did wonder if they would still have taken her home if they weren't into girls but given her recent experiences with men, she could understand better the attraction of women. Back home they wouldn't have been able to be so open about their relationship. Dinosaurs like Dimitry would have insulted them if he saw them holding hands in the street.

Afina's mother had transferred a thousand euros to Emma's bank account, which Afina knew was probably all of her life savings. They had investigated other ways of transferring money but Afina had no passport or means of identification, which was needed when collecting the money. It would also be necessary to go in person to collect the money, so when Emma had suggested transferring the money to her bank account, Afina had been quick to agree. She had no qualms about paying the money into the account of what was virtually a stranger. She completely trusted Emma and Becky.

It was Monday morning and the girls had left for work. Afina was so grateful to them for allowing her to stay in the apartment even when they weren't there. She didn't think anyone at home would be so trusting. You'd come back to your apartment at the end of the day and it would be stripped bare! Afina just couldn't face the thought of leaving the apartment. She was only ten minutes from Stefan's place and couldn't risk bumping into him or Dimitry on the streets.

Afina knew that the policewoman was dead and the policeman seriously injured. She had heard it on the radio news. The police had appealed for witnesses to come forward. She was a witness but too scared to contact the police. She was quite sure Dimitry would never allow her to give evidence and even if he was locked up, she was certain he had friends who would pay her a visit. There was also her family to consider. She was feeling guilty both about having to ask her mother for money she could ill afford to give her and potentially putting them in danger of reprisal from Stefan for her running away.

During the day, Afina cleaned the apartment from top to bottom. She felt it was the least she could do in return for being made so welcome. When the girls came home they thanked her and suggested they should all go out for a drink after dinner. Afina wasn't keen on the idea and the girls quickly understood she was worried she might bump into her assailant.

"We're just going to our local favourite pub," Becky stressed. "It will be perfectly safe. You don't normally get many men and if you do they're gay."

Afina realised Emma and Becky would frequent pubs where the likes of Dimitry would never think of going. "Okay, let's go," she said.

"Great and don't worry about having no money. When our friends catch a look at you, they will be queueing up to buy you drinks," Emma said.

It took a minute for Afina to understand what Emma meant and then she smiled shyly. "I like girls but not in that way."

"Won't stop them trying to convert you," Becky laughed.

"Can I ask a question please? Is it possible to make a call from your phone without the person I am calling seeing the number?"

"Easy," Emma said. "Do you want me to show you how?"

"Yes please."

They went to the lounge, Emma pushed a few buttons and then handed the phone to Afina. "There you go. I've hidden the number."

"Thank you, Emma." Afina said. She waited for Emma to leave the room and then dialled nine, nine, nine.

CHAPTER NINE

Adriana was home by herself listening to music on her laptop. She enjoyed listening to the latest songs and creating playlists of her favourites. She also enjoyed the freedom of having a bedroom all to herself since Afina had left. She had stuck some posters on the wall and moved things around a bit so she felt it was now her bedroom. She'd collected the remaining evidence of it once being her sister's bedroom and stuffed everything in a single cupboard. She loved her big sister but was very pleased she had moved out so she could make the bedroom her own.

Her mother had gone shopping and wouldn't be back for at least an hour, which gave her the time to chat with some friends about the latest music in the charts. Afina had introduced her to loads of English music and she was a particular fan of Ed Sheeran. She hoped one day to see him in concert.

There was a knock at the door of the apartment. She expected it to be one of her friends so was surprised to find a stranger at her door.

"Hello. You must be Adriana," the man said with a smile on his face. "Is your mother home?"

"No, she's out shopping."

"She must have forgotten I was coming. I'll come in and wait for her to return." As he said it, he pushed past Adriana into the hallway.

"Come back later," Adriana started to say and then found the stranger had his large arm around her face and across her mouth so she couldn't call out. He pushed the front door shut with his spare hand.

"Keep quiet and you won't get hurt," the man threatened. He withdrew a large knife from inside his jacket and held it close to her face. "You're a pretty girl, just like your sister. It would be a pity to spoil your looks. I'm going to let go of you now. Nod if you promise not to cry out."

Adriana nodded and he removed his arm from around her face but he kept hold of her hair.

"What do you want?" she asked in a trembling voice.

He returned the knife to his pocket and removed a piece of paper. "Tell Afina to call Stefan on this number urgently. Otherwise, I'll be paying you a return visit and I won't be so gentle." He pushed the paper into her jeans pocket and she could feel his fingers stroke her thigh through the inside of the pocket. Then he placed his free hand between her legs and rubbed

He leaned towards her and crushed her lips in a powerful kiss. She couldn't escape as he still had hold of her hair and roughly forced her head forward for the kiss. He took hold of her hand and forced her to feel his growing erection while continuing to force his tongue into her mouth.

"If I have to call again, next time I'll be fully enjoying that young body of yours," he threatened, breaking off the kiss and freeing her hand. He reached out and squeezed her breasts. "Very nice," he leered, then turned and left. "Make sure she calls," he shouted over his shoulder.

Adriana slumped to the floor and cried with relief as much as anything. She had expected to be raped.

Powell didn't have to wait long to hear back from Brian Cooper. It was just a couple of hours later when his phone rang with a withheld number.

"Powell," he answered.

"Hello, Powell. It's been a long time."

The voice was instantly recognisable. A crisp public school accent developed in prep school and refined at Eton and Oxford. He came from money and by all accounts upset his family by refusing to follow the family tradition of a career in the army, choosing instead to do his fighting in the shadows with MI5.

They had joined the service at the same time and been on the same training courses. Both of them had been recruited at University, in Powell's case that was Warwick where he'd studied Chemistry. It had been fortuitous when he was approached because he had no idea what career to follow. He knew he didn't want to be sat at a desk doing research. Why he was picked out, he never knew but he had been well chosen as he excelled at the training for his new role.

Despite Brian's privileged background, Powell had found him very down to earth and they became firm friends. Brian had the sharper mind but Powell definitely had the edge in Fieldcraft. Later in their careers they made a good team.

"Brian, thanks for calling back so quickly."

"You mentioned Bella. She is my goddaughter you know, even though I haven't seen her for almost twenty years." There was a hint of accusation in Brian's voice.

"It was best that way," Powell replied. "I'm afraid I have bad news, Brian. Bella's dead."

Powell could sense the shock at the other end of the line.

"What happened?"

"She joined the police a year ago and was stabbed a couple of days ago while out on patrol."

"Oh my God! Was she the young constable I heard was killed in Brighton?"

"Yes. Seems she was caught up in a domestic of some sort. The police have a picture of the killer but haven't found him yet."

"And you want me to help you find him? Powell, I know how you must be feeling but I can't be party to you murdering someone."

"I am not looking to kill him. That wouldn't be Bella's way."

"But it is your way, Powell. After what happened with Vanessa, I can't be party to anything similar."

"That was a long time ago. I'm not the same man. I just want to help the police find this scum. I swear on Bella's life I will not harm this man if humanly possible." Even as Powell said the words he wasn't sure it was the truth. He didn't know if he confronted Bella's killer whether he would be able to control his rage.

"I'll take a look at the reports and see what I can find out. Then I'll give you a call and an update on police progress," Brian promised. "Give me a few hours."

"Thanks, Brian. We should meet for a drink so you can update me in person. I'll come up to town."

"That would be good. I'm really sorry about Bella, Powell. Is there anything else I can do to help?"

"Not right now, thanks. Let's just make sure everything possible is being done to find her killer."

"Speak soon," Brian said and ended the call.

CHAPTER TEN

Afina called her mama to give her the phone number of the new mobile she had purchased. It had been the cheapest they sell and she had added only the minimum credit of ten pounds but it was a lifeline to home in an emergency.

As soon as her mama answered, Afina could tell there was a problem. By the end of the call, Afina realised she was facing a terrible dilemma. It was go back to Stefan and let men use her body or see her teenage sister taken and be raped, maybe even worse. There really was no choice. She loved Adriana far too much to put her through the ordeal she had endured. At least she had been with quite a few boys before she encountered Stefan and Dimitry. She was pretty sure Adriana was still a virgin and she may never recover from such an experience.

There was also her mama to consider. She would never survive something terrible happening to her baby girl. Afina had needed to be grown up at a young age and her mother often relied on her to babysit her little sister. Adriana was spoilt but Afina was in no way jealous. She had always felt protective towards Adriana.

Afina had taken down Stefan's number and sworn to her mama that there would be no more visits to her home. She would call Stefan immediately and that would be the end of the problem. Her mama wasn't entirely convinced and wanted to know why this Stefan needed Afina to call so urgently. What had Afina done? Her mama was sure she had done something wrong but Afina simply said it was all a misunderstanding. She had stayed with him and left without paying for her room when her bag was stolen. Now she had her mama's money she could repay him and the problem would go away.

After the call, Afina went to her bedroom and cried, not for herself but for Adriana and her mama. She could only imagine the fear Adriana had felt when the man came to the apartment. She would have been terrified. Afina had recently experienced similar fear and been lucky enough to escape but Adriana would not be able to run away. There was nowhere for her to go.

Afina knew she had to be strong and to act quickly. It had been her decision alone to come to England, which meant everything that had happened since was her responsibility. Her mama had never wanted her to leave home. Therefore it was up to her to put matters right. At the very least she needed to buy some time and ensure her family were no longer in danger. She knew what she must do but still hesitated to call Stefan. She went over all the possibilities in her mind one more time. Finally, she knew she must waste no further time, summoned up her courage and dialled the number for Stefan.

After the call to Stefan, Afina told the girls she wanted to go shopping for a few new clothes. She couldn't be sure the clothes she left at Stefan's would still be there when she returned and anyway, she wanted to treat herself to something, it was the least she deserved. The girls knew all the best places to shop in Brighton and would take her to the stylish but not too expensive shops. Afina needed to both look and sound confident when she met Stefan.

Powell took the train from Brighton to Victoria and then walked the ten minutes to the Thai restaurant in nearby Belgravia, which Brian had chosen, saying it served a great value business lunch. Powell had looked up the restaurant on the internet before leaving home and it was definitely very upmarket and quite different to the pubs and restaurants they frequented twenty years earlier.

Powell arrived first and shortly after he recognised Brian enter. Powell realised people could change in twenty years but he was surprised by how much Brian had changed. He had put on several stone in weight and the once slim figure was now decidedly rotund.

"Good to see you, Brian," Powell said, standing and shaking hands.

"It's been a long time," Brian responded with a firm shake. "I'm so sorry about Bella."

They both took their seats and almost immediately a pretty waitress appeared wearing a traditional Thai dress. "Can I get you something to drink?" she asked.

"Fancy some wine?" Brian asked, looking at Powell.

"Fine with me, I came on the train."

"A bottle of the Pinot Grigio, please," Brian requested, turning back to the waitress.

Sat opposite Brian, Powell could observe the signs of aging in his old friend. The hair was grey and thinning on top, the skin lined and wrinkled. He hadn't worn particularly well.

"You're looking very fit," Brian continued, when the waitress had left.

"I took up Kick Boxing a few years ago. I'm a second Dan black belt."

"As you can probably guess from looking at me, I've had a desk job for the last ten years."

"You have put on a bit of weight," Powell acknowledged with a smile. "So can you tell me what you actually do nowadays?"

"Believe it or not, I'm Director of Training. I'm responsible for churning out more of the likes of you and me of thirty years ago."

"That's quite a change from what we used to do."

"You can't go running around undercover for ever. Irish operations were scaled down and I had the opportunity to share my experience with the new recruits. It was a lot safer and after what happened to you, I realised it was probably just a matter of time before my luck ran out, so it was quit the service or change job. Now I have a decent pension to look forward to and Linda knows I will be home on time every day."

"How is Linda?"

"She's well. She was shocked to hear about Bella. She sends her love."

"And the kids?"

"They're both doing well."

Powell couldn't help but feel a pang of jealousy for his friend's happy family life. It was part of the reason why he had lost contact. After losing Vanessa, he wanted to sever ties with the past and the job which had caused the death of the woman he loved. Brian and his family life would have been a permanent reminder of what might have been.

The waitress reappeared with the wine and took their orders. Powell was happy to see prawn red curry on the set menu and Brian chose the chicken green curry, suggesting they could share.

"So what have you been able to find out?" Powell asked.

"The local police have had a tip off that the killer in the photo is a Romanian called Dimitry. They think it probably came from the girl he was chasing but they haven't so far been able to find either of them."

"A photo and a name. Surely he shouldn't be too hard to locate."

"They think he might have already skipped the country. By the time the police checked CCTV cameras and circulated a picture, twenty four hours had elapsed. They checked flights from Gatwick and there were five men called Dimitry left in that period for Romania but of course he may have been using a different name. The police are looking at the airport cameras to try and identify whether our man was one of the five."

"Shit! Have the Romanian police been asked to check out the five suspects."

"Yes but it won't be top of their priorities and frankly, based on previous experience, expectations aren't high for a good result. It's a poor country and a little money goes a long way. And one of them paid cash for his ticket so we have no address from a credit card. If he gave a false address when buying the ticket, he will simply disappear."

Powell was thoughtful for a minute. "So we need to find where he was living in England. If he had to get out so quickly, he may have left behind something we can use to track him down."

"The local police are thinking he might have been involved with prostitution. Since they joined the EU, there has been quite an influx of Romanian working girls and their pimps. It's possible the girl he was chasing was working for him. It's even possible she had been tricked into entering the country with the promise of a false job and put to work as a sex slave."

"And this goes on in Brighton?"

"Sadly, it goes on everywhere. I've looked at the reports and the police have been around all the known brothels but found zero. I think we have to assume that even if someone knew something they would be too scared to talk."

"So you're telling me the police have hit a dead end?"

"They have a name and a picture. I would guess they will issue a European Arrest Warrant for Dimitry and hope if he has gone back home that an honest cop will spot him. There is also the girl to be found. She is an eye witness and they will need her to testify when they do find Dimitry."

"Why haven't I seen the photos all over the news?"

"I assume the police don't want Dimitry to know they have his photo. Now they know his name and the fact he's Romanian, they are probably worried if they make a big splash of what they know, he'll go to ground. This way he may think he's safe."

Their food was delivered and Powell digested what he had heard as he filled his plate. He had lost his initial confidence the police would find this Dimitry and bring him to justice.

"The food's good," Powell said. He hadn't eaten a proper meal since receiving the news about Bella.

"Best Thai in London."

"I can't just sit back and do nothing," Powell said after a while.

"I know but neither can you go looking for revenge the way you did after Vanessa. The Service won't cover for you this time. I don't want to see you end up rotting in jail."

"Don't worry, I don't fancy living out my retirement in a prison cell. Anything I discover I'll share with the police. I want justice not revenge and I won't dishonour Bella's memory and choice of career by becoming a vigilante."

"Glad to hear it, but I think you said something similar twenty years ago," Brian said unconvinced. "Then all hell was let loose."

"Twenty years is a long time. Believe it or not I've spent the time trying to be sociable with customers in my bar and I haven't spiked anyone's drink in all that time."

"Sorry to doubt you. I guess I've spent too long in this business, it's really difficult to believe anything you hear nowadays."

"I can't say I've missed it." Powell hated to think what sort of father he would have been to Bella if he hadn't left the service. He had given everything to his job and paid a heavy price for his commitment.

"It really is good to see you again," Brian said with a smile, lightening the moment.

"And you," Powell replied and meant it. "I'll let you know the arrangements for Bella's funeral. It'll be in the next couple of weeks. They have to do an autopsy first." Powell didn't like the idea of Bella being cut open but in a murder case it was unavoidable.

Brian refilled their wine glasses. "I don't know how you manage to own a bar and not be an alcoholic!"

"It was a problem in the early years but then I took up kickboxing and sorted myself out."

"And is the bar doing well?"

"I bought a nice house a few years back, drive a new BMW and the bar pretty much runs itself so I can't complain."

"Those days we spent skulking about in the shadows must seem a long way off."

"In some ways they do but as Bella was growing up, every time I looked at her I was reminded of the past. Unfortunately, I've never really been able to escape my past despite the veneer of success because I would always be willing to give it all up to be back with Vanessa… And now Bella is gone as well."

"We'll find him, Powell," Brian said with conviction. "I promise you we'll find this Dimitry."

CHAPTER ELEVEN

It was time to say goodbye to Emma and Becky. Afina kissed them both and then handed Emma an envelope.

"What's this?" Emma asked.

"If you don't hear from me by tomorrow evening, I want you to hand it to the police."

"Afina, you're not going back to him, are you?" Emma was eyeing the envelope suspiciously. "You can't go back to a man who tried to rape you."

"Look, stop worrying," Afina said, trying to sound light hearted. "I'm not going near that particular person. In fact, I hear he's left the country. I'm going to be staying with a friend from Romania."

"So what is in this letter?" Becky asked.

"It's just a precaution. If I am run over by one of your buses while trying to cross the street and looking the wrong way, I want the police to know what happened to me." Afina was struggling with the idea of cars driving on the wrong side of the road.

The girls didn't look convinced. "So where will you be staying?" Becky asked. "Give us your address."

"I can't do that but it's actually not far from here. The person I'm staying with is very private. I Promise we'll all go for a drink soon. I just need to sort some things out."

"Can we at least call you?" Emma asked.

"Of course you can, you have my number. Call me anytime you want and I promise I will call you as well."

The girls relaxed a little.

"I have to be going now, my friend is expecting me." Afina hugged and kissed each girl one more time. "I will never forget what you have done for me." She turned and hurried away so they wouldn't see her cry.

The girls waved goodbye as they watched her walk away.

Afina definitely wasn't feeling as confident as she had portrayed to the girls. She had seven hundred pounds left from the money her mama had sent but only one hundred on her, which was hidden inside her bra. She

Bill Ward

had left the remainder of the money in Emma's account. She reasoned it would be a potential lifeline if things didn't work out as planned.

Afina had arranged to meet Stefan in a coffee house on Western Road, close to where she had seen Dimitry murder the young policewoman. As she walked past, there were flowers on the side of the road marking the spot. She couldn't suppress the flashback of that night's events, said a small prayer for the girl who had been killed and increased her pace.

It took her about fifteen minutes to walk to the cafe and she arrived intentionally early. She wanted to be already seated when Stefan arrived. She ordered a latte and treated herself to a cake.

Stefan entered twenty minutes later and spotted her sitting at the table. He approached the table with a smile. "Afina, it is good to see you again," he said, as if they were the best of friends.

"I'll have another latte, please," she requested. "We need to talk before I come back with you."

Stefan seemed surprised by her confidence and stood for a moment uncertain whether to agree before realising he had no choice. It was a busy café and he didn't want to create a scene. He returned with her coffee and an espresso for himself.

"I have some rules," Afina said, once Stefan was seated.

"I think you misunderstand our arrangement," Stefan interjected sharply. "I am the one who makes the rules."

Afina ignored Stefan's interruption. "I will come back to you and fuck all the men you want, with a smile on my face. I will be so good they will all come back for more. I will literally be a fucking goldmine for you. But I will not let anyone beat me again. Neither Victor nor Dimitry are to come near me. If either of them ever puts their cock in my mouth again, I swear I will bite it off. Finally, I need some time off each week and I need to earn some money."

"And why should I agree to any of your demands?"

"Because you will make lots of money from me. I am pretty and I know what men like. You should also know that I have taken out some insurance. I have written down every detail of what has happened to me and if I ever go more than three days without contact, the letter will be given to the police. I think you understand how bad that would be for your business."

"You shouldn't have done that," Stefan said angrily.

"What am I supposed to do? Just let you use me as you want. I don't think so. For all I know, you wanted me to come back because of what I have seen and know about Dimitry. Maybe you just wanted to silence me."

"Dimitry has left the country. You will not see him again. I wanted you back because you are good business. As you say, you are pretty. Men will always pay good money for you."

"Then do we have an agreement?"

"How much money do you want?" Stefan asked.

"Fifty per cent."

"I find the customers and provide the room. A room in Brighton costs good money. I also have to make payments to the local police and others. I will give you twenty pounds for every customer who stays half an hour and thirty pounds for an hour. That is a generous offer and I will not negotiate further."

Afina was excited by the thought of making more money in a day than she could make in a month at home. "Agreed. One final point, I want to be treated with respect. I may be your whore but I am not your slave."

Stefan downed the rest of his coffee. He held out his hand. "We have an agreement. Keep the men happy and I will treat you well."

Afina shook his hand and smiled. She knew from talking to Emma and Becky what you could earn working in a bar. Working for Stefan, she would be able to earn twice as much. She still didn't trust Stefan but she was pleased to hear Dimitry was no longer around.

She felt sorry for the policewoman but she had to look after her own family. With this work she could afford to send money home every month. Within a couple of years, if she saved carefully, she would have enough money to return home and get her own apartment. She was feeling a little more positive about the future.

Emma was home alone when the two police officers knocked on the door. She'd had a very liberal upbringing by parents who, if they'd been borne a generation earlier, would have been called hippies. She had therefore inherited her parent's mistrust of authority in general and police specifically.

"What can I do for you?" Emma asked.

"I'm Chief Inspector Brown," the older man wearing a suit introduced himself and showed his identification. "And you are?"

"Emma Jackson. Why do you want to know?"

"An emergency call was recently made from this address. Were you the caller, Miss?"

Emma was genuinely surprised and confused. "We don't have any emergency."

"Can we please come in?"

Emma stepped back to allow the policemen to enter. She showed them through to the lounge. "I think you've made a mistake," she said as they all sat. "We really don't have any emergency."

"Do you live here alone, Emma?"

"No, I live with my partner."

"So it's possible he made the call?"

"My partner's name is Becky."

"Sorry, could she have made the call?"

"Look, what is this about? I can assure you neither of us have called the emergency services… And we don't make joke calls."

"Has anyone else been in your house in the last couple of days?"

Emma couldn't hide her sudden realisation of who must have placed the call. "There was one girl here for a short time. Her name was Afina. She told us she had been nearly raped so we invited her back for a drink. I suggested we order her a taxi but she didn't want us to and just before she went, she asked to use the phone. She also asked me to show her how to block the caller ID. I had no idea she was calling the police but I guess it makes sense."

The chief Inspector took a photo from his pocket and asked, "Is this the girl you know as Afina?"

It was a bad photo but it was definitely Afina. "That's her," Emma confirmed.

"Can you tell me how I can contact this Afina?"

"Is she in trouble?"

"Is that relevant?"

"I suppose not. I'm sorry but I have no idea how to contact her. We were just playing good Samaritans and she was very private. We suggested her calling the police but she said it wasn't necessary so I don't understand what changed her mind. She left yesterday morning."

"So you're certain you have no way of contacting her again?"

"None, sorry. She didn't even own a phone." Emma wasn't going to give them any extra information. She wasn't sure what had truly happened to

Afina but if she wanted the police to help, she would ask.

"Did she say where she was from? Afina doesn't sound like an English name."

"She said she was from Romania."

The Chief Inspector adopted his most serious voice and said, "We believe her life may be in danger so if you hear from her again, please contact us immediately." He handed across a card with his contact details. "Any time, day or night, ring me immediately if you hear from her."

"Okay, I will," Emma agreed but had no intention of doing anything of the kind.

She was wondering what was in the letter Afina had written and left in her care. She was fairly certain Afina hadn't told her and Becky the whole truth about who she was running from the night they found her or why she was moving out. However, she had called and said everything was okay as she promised.

The Chief Inspector interrupted her thoughts. "I have to go now but my Detective Sergeant is going to stay behind and take a detailed statement from you. He will need the same from your partner."

CHAPTER TWELVE

"I'm Danny," he said, as the girl answered the door.

"Welcome Danny, I'm Mara. Come with me."

Danny followed her up a flight of stairs and she directed him into a bedroom on the first floor. She closed the door behind them.

His immediate reaction on seeing Mara had been relief. She had the sort of dark looks he normally associated with Italian and Spanish girls, though her profile had said she was neither of those nationalities. There was no doubt however, she was the same girl he had chosen after looking at dozens of profiles online. He had wondered if the pictures were genuine or just any pretty girl and when you turned up you were met with someone rather less attractive with too much hair, but Mara more than lived up to his expectations. The research he'd done on the internet had been worthwhile.

It was the first time he had ever visited an escort or paid for sex and he was surprised by how easy it was to arrange. A call to a mobile number and he was provided the address, which was just two minutes from the Churchill Square shopping centre, where he'd just parked. He had walked past this house several times in the past and never had any idea what was going on inside.

"Is this your first time here," Mara asked.

"Yes it is." Wouldn't she remember if I had been before? Obviously not, which probably meant for her it was a bit like working on a factory line. His expectations of good sex were not high.

"How long do you want to stay?" she asked.

"An hour, please."

"That's one hundred pounds."

Danny handed over the money.

"Do you want any extras?" Mara asked.

"Such as?"

"Anal is an extra thirty pounds. Maybe you're into something kinkier like bondage?"

Danny smiled nervously. "Thanks but I just want a blowjob and sex."

"Do you want a shower?"

"I had one just before I left home but if you want me to have another, I will."

"That's okay. You get undressed and I'll be back in a minute."

Danny certainly found Mara attractive and he'd enjoy having sex with her, as long as she didn't just lie on her back like a block of ice.

He had undressed to his boxers just as Mara returned.

She smiled appreciatively as she saw Danny's body. "You're in good shape."

"For an old git you mean."

"You're not old, just mature. Actually you're a lot younger than many of the men who come here and much better looking. One of my regulars is over seventy!"

Mara closed the distance between them and kissed him lightly on the lips, which then turned into something much more passionate. She slid her hand down his shorts as she kissed him and stroked his cock. After kissing him for a couple of minutes she kneeled in front of him and removed his shorts before taking him in her mouth. He was quickly fully hard for her.

"I'll cum if you keep doing that," Danny warned.

Mara nodded encouragingly and kept sucking. For Danny it had been a long time since he'd experienced anything similar and he soon reached the point of no return.

Mara could tell he was about to cum and at the last second moved his cock away from her mouth and pointed him at her breasts.

She waited for a few seconds until he was completely finished then stood up and reached for a packet of baby-wipes on the bedside table. She started wiping herself down and passed him a couple of tissues to clean himself.

Mara propped up the pillows and lay on the bed. She patted the space next to her and Danny joined her.

"So is this the first time you ever visit an escort?" Mara asked.

"Yes it is. Was it that obvious?"

"What's your name?"

"Danny."

"Well Danny, I like you. You were a bit nervous but you have a nice body and your cock works well so I'm happy."

"I'm just a bit out of practice."

"Well get your breath for a minute and then we can try again."

"Where are you from?" Danny asked.

"I'm Romanian."

"How long have you lived in Brighton?"

"Two years."

"Do you like Brighton?"

"Yes, it's very nice."

"Are there lots of Romanians in Brighton?"

"A few."

Mara started to stroke Danny's thigh.

"Are they all like you?" Danny laughed.

"Of course not. I'm very special."

CHAPTER THIRTEEN

Afina's first day of work for Stefan had gone well. There had been five men and she had earned one hundred and forty pounds, an absolute fortune back home. All of the customers had wanted vanilla sex except one who wanted anal. He wasn't too large and he had been gentle, at least at first, so she was happy enough. She had even negotiated with Stefan for an extra ten pounds for providing anal as he charged the customers extra for it.

Most of the men had been old enough to be her father and were probably married. She wondered if their wives knew they were having sex with someone else. Probably not, but how many would care if they discovered the truth? The men often complained they weren't getting enough sex at home but still loved their wives. When she was older and married, she would not accept her partner paying someone else for sex. Money was too precious to throw it away on some momentary pleasure with another woman.

She was surprised to find men of such an age were even wanting to have sex. She thought that by about fifty, people stopped having sex. Perhaps after doing this work for a year, she would become a marriage guidance councillor and teach women how to keep their men happy in bed.

During a quiet spell in the afternoon she had gone downstairs to see Mara. They had a coffee and talked about home and laughed about men and some of their stranger sexual desires.

"How long have you been doing this?" Afina asked.

" In England about two years, before that another five years."

"That's a lot of fucking," Afina laughed.

"Sure is! I've seen every shape and size of cock imaginable."

"Have you ever had a really huge one, like you see in porn movies?"

"There was one guy had a cock as long as my arm."

"Oh My God! Did you have sex with him?"

"Yes, we went at it very slowly with loads of lube."

"What was it like?"

"More pain than pleasure. I was lying there hoping he wasn't going to tear me and put me out of work for weeks."

"Do you ever get any good looking men you actually fancy?"

"Not many but there have been a few. Actually I saw a nice guy yesterday. He was older but he had a great body. I tell you what. If he comes again and I think he will, I'll see if I can get him to have a threesum with us."

"If we have a threesum, do I have to… you know… do it with you?"

"Would that be so terrible?" Mara asked mischievously. "I would go down on you better than any man ever has."

"It's just I've never done it before with a girl."

"Don't worry, you can just concentrate on the guy. Anyway, it may never happen."

"How many other girls does Stefan have working in the building?"

"Afina, I like you but you ask too many questions. It is Stefan's business and I don't talk about Stefan's business with anyone but Stefan. Most of the girls come and go quite quickly so you don't have time to make friends. But I'm always here and Stefan tells me you will be staying so we can be friends."

"I'd like that," Afina confirmed. Then added, "But I won't be your friend if you ever beat me again like that."

"There's always a new girl passing through we can volunteer for the pleasure. Victor especially likes trying the new girls."

Afina decided to change the subject. Though she had no wish to ever endure Victor again, neither was she comfortable with the thought some other girl was going to have to go through the same experience. Afina hoped she would never be asked to beat another girl for Victor's pleasure. She liked Mara but she also recognised they were very different.

CHAPTER FOURTEEN

Powell had been sent the photos of both Dimitry and the girl, who the police now had reason to believe was called Afina. He found it very hard staring at the face of his daughter's killer for the first time. It was a face he would never forget. A face he knew would haunt him in his dreams until he'd been brought to justice. Powell was used to studying and interpreting faces. This was the face of a stocky, dark man in his late thirties with the arrogance to believe he was somehow superiors to others. A man who had no qualms about killing an innocent, young woman. He would kill again if he wasn't stopped and had probably killed before. Bella wouldn't have been the first time. Powell would never be able to rest until he had looked in those dark eyes and told him that he was the father of that young girl he stabbed. Then Dimitry would know there would be no compassion, no mercy.

The girl in the photo was young, probably no older than Bella and she was pretty like Bella. She was skinnier and had different colour hair but like Bella she deserved more than life had so far dealt her. He prayed she was alive, that Dimitry hadn't found her later and killed her. Powell resolved that, as important as it was to bring Dimitry to justice, he also needed to find this girl and ensure she was safe. Bella had died saving this girl from possibly a similar fate. Bella's death would be for nothing if he couldn't find this girl and help her. That she needed help, he was in no doubt.

The newspapers, both local and national, had been calling, pestering him for interviews and wanted pictures and his life story but he had told them all to leave him alone to grieve. The last thing he wanted was his picture appearing in any newspapers. He had grown older but was still recognisable after twenty years. Some people had long memories.

Powell had decided to visit the spot on Western Road where Bella was killed. His head told him he didn't expect to learn anything new but his heart still had a strong compulsion to visit. It was a road he regularly travelled by car and on foot, linking as it did his bar in Hove and Brighton town centre.

It was a warm June day and Wimbledon was in full flow. In the past he would have watched some of the tennis on television and had even been to watch a couple of times with Bella. Wimbledon always reawakened, at least for a short time, their personal rivalry on the tennis court and on warm Sunday afternoons they would play in Preston Park. Afterwards, they would go for a late roast lunch. That had been the normal way to spend a Sunday in the Summer but never again. This was not a normal summer and it was not just the dreams of the English players knocked out in the first round, which had been crushed. He realised he had no one to share anything important with any longer. There was no shortage of acquaintances but on a planet of billions of people he felt very alone.

He purchased a bunch of flowers and walked slowly and apprehensively from the car park, unsure if he would be able to identify the exact location of her death. However, as he came close to the spot, he saw dozens of bunches of flowers lining the side of the road. There was also a police sign asking for any witnesses to come forward. He placed his flowers alongside the others and read a few of the tributes that had been left. He was touched by the fact complete strangers had taken the time to leave messages of sympathy.

Powell was absorbed in reading the notes and didn't pay any notice to the pedestrians passing him by on the pavement.

"One less pig to worry about," someone said over his shoulder.

Powell turned in shock. "What did you say?"

There were three men with shaven heads and more than their share of tattoos confronting him.

"I said, it's one less pig to worry about," one of the men sneered. He was large and looked like he spent plenty of time pushing weights.

"You should be more respectful," Powell replied, standing up straight and looking the man who had spoken, in the eye. Even at six feet two inches tall Powell was still probably an inch shorter than the excuse for a human being he was facing.

"You going to make me?" the man taunted.

Days of stress were aching to escape from Powell. He knew there would be a momentary release of tension from hurting these three fools but he was torn by the knowledge it would not be what Bella would want. They were just dumb jerks.

"This is your lucky day," Powell said, retaking control of his emotions. "I don't want any trouble."

"Then perhaps you better get the fuck out of here," the major jerk replied.

Powell took a deep breath, he didn't want this confrontation. His tone was more educational than threatening. "By the time I was twenty three, our government had taught me how to kill in more ways than you can begin to imagine. I have skills that make me lethal with or without weapons. Please just walk away."

"There's three of us," the one who had done all the talking responded. The other two suddenly looked less confident. "And you're beginning to piss me off."

"If you don't leave, I can't be responsible for what happens. My daughter died here and right now I really don't feel in the mood to take any more of your crap, so please just move on."

It took a few seconds for what he had said to sink in. One of the men who hadn't previously spoken tugged at the arm of the one who had been doing all the talking. "Let's go. It was his daughter was killed."

Powell could see the major jerk's indecision. If he walked away he lost face with the other two. He was notionally the big man and he hadn't become so by walking away from a fight. Powell was ready for what he knew was inevitable. He moved his left foot forward a little and moved his right foot to point sideways, unobtrusively adopting his fighting guard.

"Bollocks," the major jerk said, and threw a punch.

Powell raised his rear leg, bent it back upon itself, pivoted and in a sudden but smooth motion snapped his leg forward, connecting with the man's jaw. The Roundhouse kick sent the man sprawling backwards before he really knew what had hit him. Powell rounded on the other two, assuming the guard position and raising his hands in a fighting stance, ready to strike but neither seemed interested in getting further involved.

In his youth he would have put them all down just for the practise but he'd seen more than his share of blood and death for one lifetime. Such actions had long since been consigned to his past. Even his kickboxing was only used in the gym. It had been suggested he could fight competitively but he wasn't interested. It had been a means to fight his demons and bring discipline back to his life not a new path to further violence.

"Take your friend and just go," Powell instructed firmly

The two men helped their friend groggily to his feet and quickly moved away. Powell was surprised by the sound of hands clapping and looked around to notice for the first time that there were several people watching him, who had broken into applause for his actions. He decided it was time to make himself scarce and he walked away in the opposite direction to that which the three troublemakers had taken, smiling pleasantly at those who had been clapping. He noticed one man raise his camera as if to take a photo and quickly covered his face with his hand before increasing his pace. He didn't want to draw any further attention to himself.

CHAPTER FIFTEEN

Powell awoke from the dream sweating profusely. Such dreams had become very rare over the last fifteen years but this was the second consecutive night he had endured the same nightmare. Last time the dreams were regular, he had resorted at first to whisky to send himself into bed in a stupor but when that didn't work he turned to kick boxing, trying to tire himself out to such an extent he would sleep peacefully. The frequency of the dreams had gradually diminished but he wasn't sure if it was down to the exercise or just passing of time, which he found made all memories, good and bad, fade.

They had come to his house in the middle of the night. There were three of them and they hadn't bothered with subtlety. They blew open the front door and entered with automatic weapons. Powell had immediately reached for the gun in his bedside drawer and turned to tell Vanessa to call for help but she wasn't there.

He heard the men running up the stairs and knew he had only seconds to act. He threw open the door of his bedroom and instantly fired, desperate to attract the attention of the intruders. He shot the first man he saw but the others were spraying automatic fire in every direction. He threw himself to a prone position and shot a second man.

The last man threw himself through the nearest door for safety, which happened to be Bella's bedroom. Powell heard the scream and he rushed to the doorway. The man turned towards him and fired. Powell shot him as he was turning and caught him in the shoulder but as he fell he was still randomly firing. Two more bullets from Powell in the chest brought an end to the firing.

Powell rushed to Vanessa, who was lying in bed next to Bella. He called to her but she didn't respond and all he could hear was Bella screaming. In his dream Vanessa turned to him with an accusing face and told him he was too late.

In reality, she hadn't moved and a random bullet had shot her through the heart as she shielded Bella's body from the gunman. Bella was desperately trying to wake her mother until Powell scooped her up in his arms and held her tight. He reached out with his hand and felt Vanessa's neck for a pulse but there wasn't one.

Powell had known who the men were and why they were breaking into his house intent on murder. What he didn't understand was how they had found him. There had been a price on his head for six months, ever since he killed the youngest son of a senior Republican in Belfast. Word had been received from informers that the father would not rest until Powell and all his family were dead, so it had been decided he should return to the UK for a period of time, partly so he could protect his family but he had failed.

It had taken him three months to track down the man who had ordered the attack and he exacted a lingering revenge on him and his equally vile brother. Normally, it would have been easy to cover up but he had ignored a direct order not to pursue the man. It was 1994 and the IRA ceasefire had only been in force for one month, and the government didn't want him putting it at risk because of a personal vendetta. But the service wasn't married to Vanessa and hadn't lost the love of their life. Nothing and certainly nobody could have deflected him from his purpose. Afterwards, the Service had cleaned up the mess because they didn't want the IRA finding out a member of MI5 was responsible.

Although he came close to being thrown out of the Service and possibly even prosecuted, some compassion had been shown and he'd been allowed to retire early on the grounds he needed to bring up his daughter, which meant he kept his hard earned pension.

He'd left London, wanting to make a clean break with the past and settled in Brighton, cutting off all ties to the Service and his former life. His sole motivation became the need to protect Bella from any further possibility of danger. There was always the small possibility someone would come looking for revenge. The two dead brothers each had a son still alive, who might choose to ignore the ceasefire and go hunting for their fathers' killer. Powell had left no evidence of his retribution but he would be high on any list of suspects if the cousins had an ounce of sense.

He had found himself ill equipped for any new career that would allow him to bring up his daughter, which didn't involve some aspect of security or investigation work. Eventually, he made a list of everything he enjoyed doing and very high on the list was eating and drinking, so he purchased a small bar in Hove with an apartment over and built a good business. At first, he would eye up every unfamiliar face entering the bar, wondering if they were a threat but as the years passed so he reasoned did the danger. It didn't stop him taking precautions but they had become habits so ingrained he didn't even recognise his actions as out of the ordinary.

As Bella grew up, she helped with everything from washing up to serving behind the bar. It had been the location for numerous birthday parties, including her eighteenth. In a few months Bella would have been twenty one and not long after Powell was going to reach half a century. When he decided to name the bar after his baby daughter, he could never have foreseen how it would haunt him later in life to see her name in large lights every time he came to work.

He had immediately closed the bar after Bella's death and would probably have never opened it again but he had realised after a couple of days it wasn't fair to all the staff, who didn't deserve to lose their jobs, so he had quickly promoted his assistant manager Neil to manager, confident he was capable of keeping the business running.

The bar was the last thing on his mind though as he took a shower. He was sure Vanessa would stay in his dreams until this Dimitry was found. Time had been his friend once, easing the pain of guilt he felt for Vanessa's death but now it was his enemy and he needed to move quickly before the trail went cold and Dimitry disappeared into the ether.

CHAPTER SIXTEEN

Afina was getting used to the routine of her new life. Some days were relatively quiet and others, especially the weekend, she could have as many as six men in one evening. Her record in twenty four hours stood at nine men but she was already beginning to lose count of how many men she had seen in total. Men would come as late as two in the morning after they had been out drinking and clubbing. If someone had told her a few weeks ago it was possible to do what she was now doing on a daily basis, she would have scoffed at the suggestion.

She had come to realise she actually preferred the older men. They were generally polite and often charming, treating her like they would a younger girlfriend, with friendliness and respect. Many of them were just lonely and wanted some affection. She was learning how to encourage them to chat, reducing the actual time spent having sex. She sent them all away with a smile on their face.

Some of the younger men turned up drunk and could be more difficult. They expected her to suck their cock for literally every minute of the hour for which they paid. No girl could do that without getting lockjaw and though in theory they could cum as many times as they wanted, she didn't enjoy having to give a blowjob and them finishing after just five minutes, before trying to see how many times they could possibly cum in an hour to make sure they had their money's worth.

From a short time ago, when she had only ever had sex with white Romanians, Afina had now experienced many different nationalities and colours of skin. She had learned men were generally alike despite these superficial differences. What they enjoyed when naked was not dictated by their colour or nationality. If she ever applied for a job at the United Nations she thought her multi-cultural experience would prove very useful.

Despite the negatives, Afina wasn't complaining. She had sent her first money back home and been out one Monday evening with Emma and Becky to their favourite bar again, where she was indeed popular and as she wasn't looking for a boyfriend she preferred the gay bar. She had zero wish to meet a boy, even a nice one, who might want to have sex with her. Sex was now her job. She had no wish to have sex on her time off.

Stefan entered her room. They were getting on okay because she was working well and already some customers were making return visits.

"I have a customer who wants a threesum and Mara is busy so I need you to work with a girl called Lia."

It was the moment Afina had been dreading. Was she going to be expected to beat this Lia?

"Don't worry, it isn't Victor," Stefan quickly added, sensing Afina's reluctance. "It's just a normal threesum."

"Thank God," Afina replied, relieved. In fact she was so relieved that for a second she forgot she had never had a threesum before and for her there was no such thing as a normal threesum.

"She'll be here in five minutes," Stefan continued. "The customer is due in ten. Please don't discuss the details of our business arrangement with her. Your deal is a one off."

Afina was intrigued by the idea of meeting a new girl. So far she knew only Mara, despite occasionally hearing the sounds of people moving about upstairs in other rooms. Stefan had forbidden her from venturing upstairs where Mara said there were a couple of unpleasant men minding the girls, who were just passing though. Afina had no intention of mentioning her arrangement with Stefan but she would like to know more about Lia and how she came to be working for Stefan.

Lia was quiet when she entered the apartment and very nervous. She was obviously uncomfortable around Stefan. She was wearing just her underwear so Afina thought it safe to assume she was another girl living in the building. She was a pretty girl with long dark hair and larger breasts than Afina. She had a young face and Afina thought she was probably only nineteen or twenty. Afina decided to take Lia straight to her bedroom to try and get acquainted a little better before the customer arrived.

"Relax Lia," Afina said, having closed her bedroom door. "Everything will be okay."

Lia said nothing.

"Have you had a threesum before?" Afina probed.

"No."

"That makes two of us."

Lia looked up in surprise. "You've never done this before?"

"No but I think it will be fun working with someone else for a change."

"I don't want to be here," Lia blurted out. "I don't want to be having sex with dirty old men. I want to go home."

Afina was shocked by Lia's sudden outburst. "Don't say that," Afina cautioned. "Stefan might hear you and you don't want to make him mad." She realised the irony of the situation and that she was saying the same things to Lia, she had not wanted to hear from Mara.

Was Lia in the same position she had been in such a short time ago? Afina's emotions were confused. She had a natural instinct to help Lia but she had to put herself and her family first. She was getting on better with Stefan and life was improving. She wouldn't do anything that put her family at risk.

"Please help me," Lia begged.

Afina moved closer so there was no chance of being overheard. "First we must look after this customer. Then I promise I will be your friend and try to help you but we must be cautious. Do you have family at home?"

"Of course, I have my parents and my brother and sister."

"If you try to escape they will threaten your family and you will end up in a worse position."

"I would go to the police."

"That will not save your family. Promise me you will do nothing until we have discussed this again." Afina had no idea how she would be able to help Lia but she knew she must try. "Promise me," she demanded.

"Okay, I promise."

"Good. I will come and visit you soon but now you must smile and we must show this man a good time."

CHAPTER SEVENTEEN

Afina had quite enjoyed the previous day's threesum. The man had been pleasant and quite funny. Even Lia had relaxed a little although she needed to learn to smile more often. It had been good to work with another girl and made the time pass quicker. They had shared the sex duties and when he requested they play together, Afina had seen the look of horror on Lia's face at the suggestion, so volunteered herself for the job of licking pussy. She didn't think it could be rocket science, after all most men managed okay and she doubted they were born with any innate ability in their tongues. She tried to provide what she liked receiving but had no idea if she was doing it right as Lia uttered none of the usual sounds of appreciation.

They tried a few different positions and the man left very happy and promising to return, which was all Stefan wanted to hear. Afina suggested to Lia she needed to pretend a bit harder that she was actually enjoying herself even if she wasn't. Again Afina found herself passing on the same advice she had received from Mara.

After a late breakfast of rolls with ham and cheese, Afina decided to bring up the subject of Lia with Stefan. "Can I go visit with Lia?" Afina asked. "She was a bit lonely and I think she would work better if she had a friend."

"That would have been a good idea except Lia left last night," Stefan replied.

Afina's heart skipped a beat though she wasn't entirely sure why. "Where did she go?"

"She has moved to another city. I have business interests all over the country so often the girls only spend a few days here before moving away to work elsewhere."

Afina had only known Lia for an hour but she felt she had let her down. She had promised to be her friend and now she was gone and probably more alone and scared than ever.

"I will go downstairs later and have a coffee with Mara instead then."

"Sure."

Afina washed the few dishes, had a shower, dressed and applied her makeup so she was ready to see a customer if one should arrive on short notice. She was troubled by Lia's leaving and needed to talk to a friend. She couldn't share anything about her life with Emma and Becky so that only left Mara.

Afina suggested they walk to the nearby Starbucks, saying she needed some fresh air and as she offered to but the coffees, Mara was happy to agree but they would have to get takeaways and bring them back to the apartment, in case a customer turned up. Mara called Stefan and let him know they would be gone about twenty minutes.

They walked slowly and Afina came straight to the point. "I had a threesum with a girl called Lia yesterday."

"You did! Tell me about it."

"Do you know Lia?"

"No but I told you, many girls only stay a few days."

"Why is that?"

"Questions, questions! Always questions! Tell me about your threesum. Did you enjoy it?"

"I'll give you all the gory details if you tell me why the girls spend so little time here and where they go."

"Okay, I give up. Stefan brings them into the country and then he sells them to men who put them to work in different parts of the country."

"He sells them!" Afina was shocked. Was she one of the girls who should have been sold if she hadn't run away?

"Yes. I have overheard some conversations. I think he receives about fifty thousand pounds for each girl."

"This is madness! They are human beings. You can't just buy and sell people."

"We are the lucky ones."

"Why doesn't he sell you?" Afina asked.

"He keeps you and me because we make him good money. He can't keep all the girls. There isn't room so he sells them on… Now tell me about your threesum."

"Just one more question. Where is Dimitry?"

"I don't know. I haven't seen him for ages."

"Do you know I saw him murder a policewoman. She was no older than me."

Mara looked shocked. "Afina, you mustn't say anything. They would kill you."

"Stefan knows I saw everything."

"Then I don't understand why you are still alive?"

"I have some insurance. I have written down what I saw and left a letter with a friend who will give it to the police if she doesn't hear from me. I also promised to continue to work for him in return for them not hurting my family."

"So you have a Mexican standoff. You know too much but they have threatened your family."

"Yes."

"You are not safe, Afina. Stefan is more reasonable but Dimitry might just kill you and your family because he is pissed with you. Then he will come back to the house to fuck some girls and not give a damn about what he has done. He is not human, Afina. You need to think seriously about your future. I don't want anything to happen to you."

Afina felt her new found confidence crumbling. "But Dimitry has surely gone back to Romania. He is in hiding."

"Maybe or maybe he will change his looks and return with a different name and passport. He won't just walk away from this business or forget about you. He and Stefan make too much money. I think he has told Stefan to keep you close so he knows where to find you when he wants you."

Afina realised she had not thought of every possible scenario when she came back to work for Stefan. What Mara said made sense. They were at Starbucks so ceased talking and ordered their coffees.

"You've never told me how you came to work for Stefan?" Afina asked, as they started back towards the apartment.

"It was my choice," Mara answered. "I didn't come here like the other girls and you. I wanted to make money and Stefan is my cousin."

"Your cousin!"

"Don't worry. He's my cousin but you are my friend. I won't tell him anything you tell me. Now enough questions and enough about Stefan. It is your turn to answer my question. Tell me about your threesum. Did you lick this Lia's pussy?"

CHAPTER EIGHTEEN

Danny called and arranged to see Mara for a threesum. He said he would leave her to choose a suitable second girl for their afternoon adventure but he liked girls with long hair and long legs, if she knew such a girl. He had mixed feelings about the meeting when he rang the doorbell. The presence of a second very attractive girl was on the one hand hugely exciting but he was also nervous. His hopes were raised high and that could always lead to a crashing disappointment.

Mara answered the door and led him to the same bedroom. She took his two hundred pounds for the hour and promised to return shortly. When the door opened and the two girls entered he was ecstatic to see Afina. She was exactly what he had hoped for and he was almost lost for words.

"Hello, I am Afina."

"Did I choose well?" asked Mara.

"Perfect," Danny replied. "You both look stunning."

The girls started running their hands over his chest and down his legs. Mara kissed him and then Afina took a turn. Mara knelt and pulled down Danny's boxers.

"I bet Danny would love to have both of us suck his cock at the same time," Mara suggested.

Afina knelt beside Mara and together they both licked and sucked him. Danny tried to prolong the pleasure but lasted only about five minutes. This time Mara directed Danny's cum all over Afina's breasts.

"Lie back Danny and enjoy the show," said Mara, handing him a couple of wipes.

"Can I have some wipes, please," Afina asked Mara.

"You don't need them," Mara replied. "I'm going to clean you up."

She took Afina in her arms and started to lick and clean Danny's cum from her breasts.

Afina was uncertain at first but as Mara found her nipples and began teasing them with her tongue, she knew she wanted more. Afina glanced at Danny and saw his eyes were about to pop out of his head. Mara spent several minutes ensuring there was no remaining cum on Afina. She then kissed her fully on the lips. Afina had kissed a couple of girlfriends for a laugh in the past but not with the passion Mara was showing.

"Why don't you lie next to Danny," Mara suggested.

Afina lay next to Danny and he immediately started kissing her. She then felt Mara's soft lips on her thighs and her legs parted, an invitation Mara was quick to accept.

For Afina, the next half an hour was a blur of entangled legs, kisses and pleasure with her not always sure whether it was Mara or Danny she was feeling. She made both of them smile more than once when she assumed a couple of flexible positions only a gymnast would achieve.

When Danny cried enough, Mara offered him a soft drink and he requested water, which she went to fetch.

"I really like you, Afina," Danny said. "Could I come and see just you the next time?"

"Of course but didn't you like our threesum?"

"I loved it but I'm not super rich and a threesum is just for special occasions. I like Mara as well but it would be nice to just spend some time with you."

Afina was flattered by Danny's request because she considered Mara far prettier. "Just call the same number you called before and ask to see me, Afina. I'm nearly always available."

Mara returned with the water for Danny. "I thought you might be having a quickie without me," she laughed.

"You've worn me out," Danny answered. "I've never experienced anything like that before."

"I hope you enjoyed it?" Mara asked.

"Hated every minute of it!"

"So you won't be coming again?"

"I think I've cum enough for one day, that's for sure," Danny joked."

Danny dressed and kissed both girls on each cheek before leaving. He knew he would be back again very soon.

After a shower, Afina went back to her room and lay on her bed thinking about Mara. She was fairly certain that Mara was bisexual. It had not just been an act for the customer. Mara had enthusiastically gone down on her and almost begged her to do the same in return. Over the last few days, Afina had also spotted Mara looking at her from time to time in a slightly strange manner. Afina had just dismissed it as being curiosity but now she wondered if it meant something more. Perhaps Mara was smitten by how she looked and had developed something of a crush. Afina hoped she could use that to her advantage, that and the fact she was Stefan's cousin. She wouldn't do anything to hurt Mara but she recognised Mara was happy with her lifestyle. Mara would not go out of her way to help the girls being sold as sex slaves. Afina on the other hand was going to have to do something. She just didn't know what.

CHAPTER NINETEEN

Powell had been informed Bella's body was available for a funeral as the autopsy was finished. A senior police officer had telephoned him and asked if it would be all right to have a ceremonial funeral service in memory of Bella, as she had been killed in the line of duty. The officer had also mentioned that she was being nominated posthumously for an award for outstanding bravery.

Powell was happy to have a special service and indeed felt it was the least Bella deserved. The service was to take place at St Andrew's Church in Hove, which was the same place where Bella had been Christened. He wasn't very religious by nature but it had always been Vanessa's wish to have Bella christened and out of respect to her memory, it had been one of the first things he did after moving to Hove. Now here he was, just a few years later, facing her memorial service. What he had experienced during his lifetime made it difficult to believe in a benevolent God. The ceremonial service was to take place in the morning and then in the afternoon there was to be a much smaller service at the Woodvale Crematorium in Brighton, which was just for close family and friends.

Powell was shocked and pleased by the turnout at the church. There were hundreds of mourners on the road around the church and inside was packed. There were even television cameras at the entrance to the church and many photographers, which Powell did his best to avoid. A Lifetime spent avoiding cameras wasn't going to change now. Everywhere senior officers could be seen in very smart attire. Various local dignitaries introduced themselves and offered their condolences prior to the service starting.

Bella's coffin was carried into the church by six of her colleagues. The Chief Constable of Sussex spoke eloquently about Bella and the sacrifice she had made. Powell was deeply affected by the whole service and tears flowed down his cheeks. It was almost too much to bear and the only thought that sustained him was the need to find the man responsible.

After the cremation, family and friends had been invited back to the bar.

Powell took Brian aside and asked him if there was any update in the search for Dimitry.

"The police have found him on the CCTV at Gatwick so we now know for sure he has left the country." Brian reported. "But there's nothing positive coming back from Romania."

"Shit!" It was the worst possible news.

"Powell, please promise me you won't go chasing after him. Leave it to the police to find him."

"I will give the police every opportunity to find him first. But if I think they are getting nowhere then you can't expect me to do nothing. Bella meant everything to me."

"I understand. Please just be careful... On a more positive note I hear Constable Myers is going to live. Seems the knife just missed his vital organs and despite losing a lot of blood he should make a full recovery. He was very lucky."

Powell knew he should be happy for the policeman and his family but he could only think that he wished it was Bella alive and Myers who had been the unlucky one.

Powell noticed both Bella's grandmothers were circulating with trays of food and drinks, as if keeping busy somehow made the whole occasion more bearable. In a similar vein, he spotted Chief Inspector Brown chatting to some other officers and decided to check if he had any further news.

"Thanks for coming, Chief Inspector," he said. "Might I have a word?"

"Of course." The Chief Inspector excused himself from his companions and followed Powell to a quieter corner of the lounge.

"Any update, Chief Inspector? Are you making progress with finding my daughter's killer?"

"We are doing everything possible," the Chief Inspector said encouragingly. "We are pursuing a number of lines of enquiry."

"I'm sure you are but are you any nearer finding Bella's killer?"

"I'm sorry but as I've told you before, I really can't discuss the details of the case with you Mister Powell."

"It's just Powell," he snapped. Then in a more pleasant tone he asked, "Do you expect an arrest anytime soon?"

"This is a murder enquiry, Powell. You can't expect miracles."

"I gave up believing in miracles many years ago. I just want to hear you are making progress."

"Well we have definitely made progress."

"Can I help further in any way? For example, would it help if I was to offer a reward for information?"

"To be honest I'm not sure it would at the moment. It might actually bog the enquiry down pursuing a load of false leads. But let me think on it further and if circumstances change we can discuss it again."

Powell walked away feeling a mixture of anger and helplessness. He went behind the bar and found a bottle of his favourite malt whisky. He poured an extra-large measure, picked up the bottle and headed upstairs to Bella's apartment.

He sunk in the soft armchair and downed his drink in one before refilling the glass. The warmth from the whisky quickly spread throughout his body and he relaxed. He was glad to be away from the people downstairs, who were full of sympathy but he didn't want to hear anyone else tell him how sorry they were for his loss. What did they know? They hadn't dedicated their lives to bringing up Bella. They hadn't seen her through the ups and downs of life.

He took another sip of whisky and then went to one of the cupboards and took out a photo album. He sat back in his chair and turned the pages, which transported him back in time to her first day at school, her birthday parties and the memories of happy holidays. Tears were streaming down his cheeks. There would be no new memories, no new photos to put in the album.

He had learned a long time ago life was unfair to many people but surely he had experienced more than his share of misfortune. He had lived for Bella and now she was gone. There was no meaning to his life without Bella. He didn't want to live any longer, he wanted to be with Bella and Vanessa. He finished his drink and poured another large measure.

"Thought you might be up here," Brian said.

Powell turned in surprise. "Brian, I came up here to be alone."

"Great minds think alike," Brian said, holding up another bottle of whisky and two glasses. He didn't wait to be invited but sat himself in the chair opposite Powell. He poured himself a drink. "To Bella," he toasted.

"Bella," Powell responded, raising his glass.

"You need to get back downstairs in the minute," Brian said. "People are missing you. They want to know you are all right."

"Of course I'm fucking not all right," Powell was beginning to slur his words. "I'll never be all right again."

"I can't imagine what it's like to lose one person you love let alone two like you have but you still have a lot of life ahead of you and you can't spend it getting drunk. I didn't really know Bella but I knew Vanessa and if her daughter was anything like her, then she'd be begging you to get up from this chair, go speak with her friends and then find a new purpose in your life until you can be with them both again."

"That's the problem. I don't believe I will ever see them again. I gave up on religion a long time ago."

"I know Vanessa and Bella believed in you and I remember a time when many others put their faith in you and you didn't let them down. So we are going to have one more drink, then we're going downstairs and after everyone has gone we'll get very drunk and remember the past but starting tomorrow, you are going to keep doing whatever it takes to bring Bella's killer to justice."

"You told me to do nothing, to leave it to the police."

"Yes but I didn't believe for one minute you would listen to me."

Afina had arranged to meet Emma and Becky for another evening of drinks. It was the second such occasion and she hoped it might become a regular event. Afina looked forward to their company and seeing some of their gay girlfriends, who had been so friendly the last time. For a few hours her life would seem more normal.

She had arranged with Stefan that on Mondays she would finish working at seven and at eight she would meet the girls. Mara was working and would cover her customers, which made Afina happy because it meant Mara could not ask to join her, something she could never allow. Afina would enjoy going out with Mara but she could not permit her to meet Emma and Becky. When asked where she went, she would say that she liked to walk by the sea and explore the town.

"Afina, we had a visit from the police," Emma said, while Becky was getting drinks. "Did you call them when you were at our place?"

"The police! What did they want?"

"Did you call them?"

"Yes but you told me I could withhold my number so they wouldn't know who was calling."

"That's true for calling normal numbers but not the emergency services."

"I'm sorry, I didn't know that. What did you tell them?"

"That you had almost been raped, we offered you a drink and a shoulder to cry on, before you left without leaving us any contact details."

"Thank you Emma, you have helped me again."

"Are you okay, Afina? We really are worried about you."

"I am fine, honestly. Everything is good now. Actually, I have another letter for you. If you don't hear from me for a week please pass both letters to the police." Afina had added the information she gained from Mara about Stefan selling girls and mentioned Lia's plight.

"Afina, this isn't right. Are you sure you're not in trouble? It isn't normal what you're doing, leaving letters with us to hand to the cops, as if you might be killed at any time."

"Don't worry, Emma. I am perfectly safe but your streets are far busier than I am used to and if I have an accident, I want the police to know about the man who tried to rape me." Afina didn't want to worry Emma and Becky or put them in danger but she really had no choice.

Emma didn't look convinced but put the letter in her bag without further argument. "Afina, just know that if you ever need us we're here for you."

"You two look serious," Becky said, returning with their drinks.

"I was just telling Afina about our visit from the police," Emma explained.

"Is everything okay?" Becky asked.

"Fine," Emma answered.

"Good because I had a crap day at work and need to get pissed!"

CHAPTER TWENTY

Afina was pleasantly surprised when she opened her bedroom door and discovered Danny was her next customer.

"Hello, Afina. How are you?" Danny asked, with a broad smile on his face.

"I'm good. How are you?" Afina recognised the face but couldn't remember his damn name.

"Very happy to see you. I've been really looking forward to seeing you again since our last meeting."

Afina led him back to her room. "How long do you want to stay?"

"Two hours please."

Afina was surprised and happy to think she would get to spend the next two hours with a customer she actually quite liked. Her previous customers had always booked a maximum of one hour. She wasn't sure how they would fill two hours though as she remembered him completely shagged out after just one hour the last time they met.

She needed to find out his name. "What is your real name?" she asked.

"It's Danny," he confirmed.

"I always think people invent false names when they come to see me," she explained.

"I guess some do but not me."

"That will be two hundred pounds then."

Danny had stopped at the cashpoint on the way so simply handed over the crisp twenty pound notes without bothering to count them again.

"I'll just be a minute. Start getting undressed."

Afina took the money into the lounge where she gave it to Stefan and told him she would be busy for two hours. Then she went to the bathroom and checked her appearance. She was wearing the lace underwear she always chose to greet customers. She decided to take an extra rinse of mouthwash but was otherwise satisfied with how she looked.

She returned to her room and found Danny naked except for his boxers. She had learned to kiss her customer almost immediately upon re-entering the room. It made the customer feel quickly at ease and saved having to make small talk. Danny was a good kisser.

After a few moments she started to explore the rest of his body with her hands and he bent to kiss her nipples, pulling her bra down to allow him access. She took the hint and reached behind her back to remove her bra. She loved having her nipples kissed and pinched.

Afina followed a similar routine with each customer. After some kissing she knelt before them and took their cock in her mouth. Mara had given her a few tips and for giving great blowjobs she said you must always be looking your man in the eyes, which was exactly what she was now doing. Unlike Mara, she also enjoyed men finishing in her mouth. She definitely preferred it to them making a mess anywhere else on her body and most of her customers didn't bother with having real sex once they had cum in her mouth.

"Let's lie on the bed," Danny suggested.

As Afina stood up she removed her knickers before joining Danny on the bed.

Danny started by kissing her on the lips again, then moved down her body, concentrating on each nipple for several minutes before lightly kissing her thighs. As he moved his tongue to between her legs and gently circled her clit she started moaning with pleasure. With other customers she had learned they liked to hear her appreciatively moaning even if they were doing it all wrong. On this occasion her response was real.

She hadn't had an orgasm with any other customer and knew she was getting close but she wasn't comfortable about letting Danny share something so personal. She had built a wall behind which she hid her real feelings from her customers. It was the way she could survive having sex with so many strangers. To have an orgasm now would send the wall crashing down.

"That was amazing," she said, sitting up and causing him to stop what he was doing. "I need you inside me. If you don't mind?"

"Sounds a great idea."

Afina took a condom from the bedside table. "What position would you like?" she asked, as she unrolled it on his cock.

"Me on top?"

Afina lay back on the bed and moaned as he entered her, another of Mara's tips.

She liked the way Danny moved inside her, not rushing and building the sensations slowly. If she closed her eyes she could imagine she was with a real boyfriend or even better Bruno Mars, who she adored. Instead, they kissed and caressed each other while she thought about Dimitry and the poor girl he had killed. It had the result she wanted and she lost any desire to orgasm.

She liked Danny and encouraged him to thrust harder before holding him tight and asking in his ear for him to cum for her. She noticed he had his eyes closed as he grunted loudly and did as she had asked. She wondered if he too had been thinking of someone else.

He rolled off her and lay next to her panting from his exertions. "Sex is so silly," he said.

"You didn't enjoy it?" Afina asked, concerned.

"I loved it," Danny responded quickly. "But it's kind of strange and funny the noises we make and what we do."

"Yes some people make a lot of noise," Afina agreed with a smile. "But noise is better than quiet. I knew you were enjoying yourself."

"Is Afina your real name?"

"Yes it is," she responded, surprised by the question. She had never thought to use a different name.

"And you are from Romania?"

"Yes."

"You speak very good English."

"Not so good but enough."

"Whereabouts in Romania are you from?"

"Bucharest. Do you know it?"

"I've never been to Romania. Perhaps I will go one day."

"You should visit. It's a nice city," suggested Afina and put her hand to her eye fearing the appearance of a tear. She was thinking of her mama and Adriana. How long would it be before she saw them again?

"What's wrong?" Danny asked, concerned.

"Sorry, I get a little homesick sometimes." She leaned into Danny and gave him a long passionate kiss. "I feel better already," she smiled, as she broke away.

"I should have brought some wine to drink," Danny said.

Afina jumped up from the bed. "I have some in the fridge."

Before Danny could answer she was out the door and a short time later returned holding a bottle of white wine and two cups. "Sorry, I don't have any glasses," she apologised.

"Can I pay for the wine?" Danny asked.

"No, it will be my pleasure to share it with you." Then she thought to add, "But it was very cheap so may not taste very good!"

"Hey it's wine and I'm not fussy."

Afina poured the wine and carried the cups to the bed.

"Cheers," she said, offering her cup for a toast.

"Cheers," Danny responded. "What do you say in Romania?"

"Noroc."

"Noroc," Danny repeated before tasting the wine. "It's cold and dry so perfect."

Afina took some wine in her mouth and kissed Danny to share the wine. Danny then took some wine in his mouth and kissed Afina's breasts, letting the cold wine run down them before then licking it back up.

"Next time I'm going to bring two bottles of champagne," Danny said, as he sat back next to Afina. "One bottle for drinking and one for playing games with."

"That sounds like fun," Afina agreed. She liked the idea of Danny becoming a regular customer. He was sexually undemanding and polite.

"Do you mind if I ask you something personal?" Danny asked.

"You can ask but I may choose not to answer."

"Fair enough. I wondered who the man is that answers the phone when I call to see you girls. Is he your or Mara's boyfriend?"

"God no! He is Mara's cousin and owns this building."

"So he is like your boss?"

"I suppose so in some ways."

"So if I wanted to take you out for a meal or something, still paying for your time of course, would I have to ask him?"

"I can ask him." Afina liked the idea of earning money for something other than fucking. "When do you want to see me and for how long?"

"How about Wednesday evening?"

"So that's the day after tomorrow?"

"Yes. I can meet you here and we can go for dinner and some champagne, then back to my place for an hour. Say meet at seven and I return you at twelve."

"That will cost a lot of money, Danny."

"Well as I would be paying for five consecutive hours I was hoping you might give me a special price."

"Give me five minutes and I will go check with Stefan," Afina said. "And when I come back you had better be ready to fuck me again. We still have an hour left."

CHAPTER TWENTY ONE

Danny collected Afina from outside her building at exactly seven. He had been pleased when Afina came back in the room and informed him the arrangements were fine and the cost would be four hundred pounds for the five hours. As he would also have to pay for dinner and drinks it was going to be an expensive evening but he was also sure it was a worthwhile investment.

He had called her mobile to announce he was waiting downstairs and when she emerged she looked stunning in a short black dress and high heels, which accentuated her long legs. He realised it was the first time he had seen her wear anything other than her underwear.

"You look great," he said appreciatively.

"Thank you. You look very nice as well."

Danny was wearing designer jeans and jacket, which he'd chosen for being smart but not too formal. He was conscious of their age difference and wanted them to appear like a real couple. In truth, he realised it didn't really matter what he wore as he was paying for the pleasure of Afina's company.

Danny had parked right outside the house as he was only going to be five minutes, despite it being a double yellow line.

"Shall we," he said, opening the passenger door of his car.

"Wow! This is a great car," Afina said once seated.

"It's a BMW Z4 and with the local speed limit reduced to twenty miles per hour, I'd be better off driving something that doesn't make me long to be on a German motorway, every time I get behind the wheel."

"It's very luxurious," Afina said feeling the leather seat.

Danny had pulled away from the kerb and was soon heading down Western Road. After ten minutes he pulled up in front of where he had chosen for them to eat. He led the way inside and they were shown to the table in the corner, he'd especially requested.

"Would you like some champagne?" Danny asked as soon as they were seated.

"That would be lovely. This is a nice place."

Danny ordered a bottle of Laurent Perrier Rose and watched Afina as she studied the menu.

"Have you eaten here before?" Afina asked.

"Many times."

"What would you recommend?"

"The Sea Bass is excellent if you like fish. That's what I'm having."

"Okay, then I will have the same."

Danny kept the glasses topped up and halfway through the main course the bottle was empty so he ordered a second bottle.

"I'm feeling a little tipsy," Afina admitted. "I'm not used to drinking champagne. The bubbles keep getting up my nose."

"I used to know someone about your age who loved drinking champagne."

"Who was that?"

"My daughter. This place is named after her in fact."

Afina look confused. "Why did someone name this place after your daughter?"

"Actually it was me who decided on the name. I own this place."

"Really! Why didn't you tell me? So your daughter is called Bella?"

"She was. Unfortunately she was a police officer and someone stabbed her in Brighton last week. Quite near where you work actually."

Afina's face went pale white. Her eyes confirmed what Powell had known since he first saw her, she was the girl in the picture being chased by Dimitry.

"I'm so sorry," Afina said quietly, obviously in shock. She reached for her glass and took a large drink. "I don't know what to say," she continued.

"You can start by telling me who is Dimitry."

"Danny, what do you mean? Who is Dimitry?"

"My name isn't Danny, its Powell. I assume it was you who telephoned the police with his name?"

Afina was lost for words. The shock of everything mixed with the champagne had left her reeling. "Danny, I mean Powell, I don't know what you are talking about. You are scaring me. I think I want to leave now." Afina started to stand up.

Powell took the grainy photo of Afina from his inside jacket pocket and handed it to her. "We have cameras everywhere in Brighton. We have one of Dimitry as well."

"I want to leave," Afina insisted.

Powell reached across and took Afina by the wrist. "If you leave here before I'm finished with you, it will be to visit the police station," he said sharply.

Afina sat back down. "Please, I can't help you," she pleaded. "I don't care what they do to me but they will kill my family. I have a mother and sister."

Powell hadn't considered that Afina might have family who were in danger. "Why do you think they will harm your family?" he asked in a gentler tone.

"Someone twice visited their home in Bucharest. The second time he scared my sister and threatened her. He said next time he would rape her and she is only sixteen. I know what these men are capable of."

"I don't understand why they don't just kill you?"

"I have some insurance and also I earn them good money."

"What insurance?"

"I have written down everything I know and left it with a friend."

"You are playing a dangerous game."

"What choice do I have?"

"Where is Dimitry?"

"I don't know for certain but probably in Romania. Why did you bring me here?"

"I needed to get you away from where you work so we can have a proper conversation."

"I don't know what to say."

"So start at the beginning and tell me everything you know about this Dimitry and why he was chasing you down a Brighton street."

CHAPTER TWENTY TWO

Powell had been shocked by everything he learned from Afina. It had made it even more difficult to let her go back to the house after they had finished talking but there was no other viable option for either of them. It was going to take time to devise a strategy to find Dimitry, while at the same time keeping Afina and her family safe. Powell had no interest in locating Dimitry if it led to the deaths of any further innocent people and neither Afina nor her family, were in any way responsible for what happened to Bella.

Powell also now understood why he had been able so easily to locate Afina and the police had achieved nothing. While she had been staying with her new friends, the police may very well have knocked on the door where she had been working but by then she was gone and when she returned they had finished their door to door enquiries. Afina also confirmed what Powell knew, her picture wasn't on the web sites advertising services. Stefan used a picture of Mara and a couple of girls who didn't exist. When customers booked a different picture but saw Afina, they never complained when told the girl was busy but Afina was available.

There had been no time or inclination for sex after their discussion. Powell was very attracted to Afina but would never have sex with her again while she was forced into having to provide sex because of her unfortunate circumstances. He was already feeling guilty about their previous sex but he was pragmatic enough not to beat himself up about something he could do nothing about. On the positive side, though he had been using Afina to get to Dimitry, now he knew her story, he was possibly the only person who could truly help her find a way out of her current predicament.

Powell recognised what Afina had told him about the trafficking and selling of girls wasn't something he could just ignore. Stefan also had to answer for his part in Bella's death because had he never brought Afina into the country, she would not have needed to escape and Bella would still be alive. Many of these girls were similar in age to Bella and that thought made him determined to do everything in his power to put a stop to the trafficking.

Powell had stayed up late after Afina left, thinking about whether he should involve the police. In the end he decided they would be likely to simply take Stefan into custody, which would put at risk any chance of finding Dimitry. Powell had promised Afina he would do nothing that would endanger her family but at the same time he needed to think about the other girls Stefan was still importing and selling. Powell didn't want to delay to such an extent that it resulted in many more girls passing through Stefan's hands and being distributed around the country, possibly never to be found again. With Dimitry in Romania and no idea if or when he might return, Powell was going to have to take action and urgently.

He had arranged to see Afina again at three in the afternoon, supposedly for a one hour session at her apartment. She had been fairly certain Stefan would be in the next room at that time and it was him, Powell really wanted to meet. Stefan would know how to find Dimitry.

Afina showed Powell to her bedroom as normal. He noticed she was less welcoming than usual and once inside the room she wrapped a towel around her body, suggesting she was suddenly self-conscious around him, wearing just her underwear.

"I have a plan," Powell announced, seated on the edge of the bed. "Here is my hundred pounds and tell Stefan I wish to speak with him."

Afina looked nervous. "What about?"

"Just tell him I wish to discuss some business."

Afina looked doubtful. "What business?"

"Look Afina, you have to trust me. I promised last night to do everything possible to protect you and your family and I keep my promises. So please go tell Stefan I wish to speak with him. And remember my name is Danny."

Afina hesitated for a second before taking the money from Powell's hand, then removed the towel and left the room. She was back just a minute later.

"Stefan is waiting for you in the lounge," Afina confirmed.

Powell smiled at Afina as he passed her before shutting the bedroom door behind him. He approached the man that was standing in the room with a slightly quizzical expression on his face.

"I'm Danny," Powell said, offering a firm handshake that was reciprocated.

"Stefan. Afina says you wanted to discuss some business with me."

"I do. I'm looking to broaden my business interests. I'm thinking you might be able to find me some suitable Romanian girls a bit like Afina. If you don't want to actually supply me directly with the girls, perhaps you could give me an introduction to someone in Romania who can help me find the right type of girls."

"Put an advert in the newspaper in Romania and you will get girls."

"I'm looking for something a bit different. I have friends who have, shall we say, rather extreme fantasies which girls do not normally want to satisfy. In fact, some of my friends find it more enjoyable when the girl doesn't want to provide what is being asked. This then gives them a reason to discipline the girls. The discipline can be very severe. My friends are willing to pay good money to spend time with such a girl, especially if she is pretty."

"I can provide your friends with everything they want. Just send them to me. I will even pay you a small commission."

"As I said, I am looking to expand my own business interests. I am able to satisfy most of my friends' other vices and I wish to be able to also provide girls. I think Romanian girls are exactly what I'm looking for as Western European girls are rather more problematic."

"So you want me to provide you with girls so you can go into competition with me? I'm not sure that is good business sense for me."

"We are satisfying different market needs and frankly, no offense but my business is aimed at a rather more upmarket clientele than your business. I am providing different services so I don't believe we will be in competition and you will make good money selling me the girls."

"I might be able to help you find the type of girls you want but they will cost a great deal of money, as much as say one hundred thousand pounds each. Do you have that sort of money?"

"I was thinking more along the lines of seventy thousands pounds for each girl."

"Such girls are not easily found and brought into the country. How many do you want?"

"I'm thinking I need three to get started. Then probably another three in about six months."

"Okay, I will provide three girls for two hundred and fifty thousand pounds. That is my final offer."

"Agreed. I will pay fifty thousand up front to cover some of your expenses and the rest is payable when I receive the girls."

Stefan smiled for the first time. "How soon do you want the girls?"

"How soon can you get them?"

"It will take about a month."

"Good. You do understand I don't want experienced working girls like Afina and Mara?"

"I understand what you want. You want nice, normal girls who won't want to be fucked up the arse by a stranger and when they resist, your upmarket customers will beat the shit out of them."

"I believe we are on the same wave length."

"Age is not important?"

"Young is good but I'm not after children, my clients are not paedophiles. And obviously the girls must be attractive as I charge a premium rate for these services."

"I will ask my friends back home to start looking for suitable girls. When can you provide the deposit?"

"Give me your bank details and I can transfer the money later today."

"You will transfer me fifty thousand pounds after just ten minutes of conversation? You are either very trusting or a fool."

"I assure you I am neither and if you are straight with me then we will both prosper. However, these fund are not just mine. I work with people in London who are investing in my new business and they would not tolerate anything adversely affecting their investment. I have made them aware of you and your business and how you can help provide the girls we want. They expect you to deliver what we purchase. The consequences of not doing so would be very bad for your business. Do I make myself clear?"

"Very clear. It is a large sum of money and it is perfectly safe with me."

"Good. You can give me your bank details and we can swap contact numbers before I leave. Now I would like to get back to Afina and finish enjoying myself."

CHAPTER TWENTY THREE

As soon as Powell had left, Afina went to find Stefan.

"What business did Danny want to discuss with you?" she asked.

"It does not concern you," Stefan replied.

"Is Danny happy with me?"

"Danny thinks you're great. Our business did not involve you. Victor is coming to see me shortly. Why don't you go find Mara and have a coffee so we can speak without distraction? If Victor sees you he may be tempted to ask to play with you again."

Afina needed no second invitation to leave. She found Mara already drinking coffee and reading a magazine.

"So tell me about last night?" Mara asked, moving to the kettle to make Afina a coffee. Did you have fun with Danny?"

"It was okay."

"Okay! I'm sure it was better than okay. While you were probably eating nice food and spending the evening with one man I was getting fucked by seven men. My pussy is damn sore this morning."

Afina smiled. "You're right," she admitted. "It was better than a normal evening. I shouldn't complain."

"So is Danny still an easy fuck or has he become kinky?"

"No, he's not very kinky."

"So why don't you look happier?"

"Sorry, I'm just a bit tired."

"I can give you some pills to help with tiredness. In fact, I can give you something to help with most conditions."

Afina was surprised. "You mean drugs?"

"I can get you anything you want."

"No thanks, Mara. It is bad enough what I am doing. I don't also want to become a drug addict."

"It can help with the work. I take some coke every now and again."

"It's not for me," Afina said with conviction.

"As you wish."

"By the way, did you know Victor is upstairs talking to Stefan?"

"Victor, so you're worried he will want a repeat performance?"

"Stefan promised me I wouldn't have to be beaten by Victor again but I'm not sure I trust him."

Mara handed Afina the cup of coffee she'd made for her. "Don't worry. There are two other new girls, I'm sure Stefan will volunteer one of them."

"And will you beat the new girl like you did me?" Afina snapped.

"I may be Stefan's cousin but if I was to upset Victor, Stefan would never forgive me. I do what I am told."

"Why is Victor so important?"

"I'm not sure but Stefan treats him like royalty. He is closer to Dimitry than Stefan. In fact I think it was Dimitry who introduced Victor to Stefan. I think he has something to do with finding the new girls and getting them in the country. He makes regular trips back to Romania and each time he returns Stefan entertains him with a girl of his choice."

"Which of them is in charge?"

"I think they are all equal. The men really in charge are back home in Romania."

"I'm not surprised Dimitry and Victor are friends. They are both equally evil."

"They are men!"

"Not all men are like those two beasts." Afina was worried to hear Victor and Dimitry were good friends. Victor would know she was responsible for Dimitry having to flee the country. She was petrified of Victor and what he might be capable of doing to her.

Powell had told her she must try to learn everything possible about Stefan and his business. Any small fact could be important. "Danny spoke privately with Stefan earlier and though I couldn't hear everything, I think Danny was asking Stefan to supply him with some girls."

"He is a greedy man. Were we not enough for him?"

"Not like that. Danny wants to go into business like Stefan."

"So that explains your bad mood. Danny is turning out to be just like other men."

"Mara, I don't understand you. You don't like men very much but you don't seem concerned that girls our age are being brought into this country against their will and forced to work as sex slaves. They are not like you, they have not chosen to do this work to make money. They have been deceived and then they are abused. How can you not want to do something to stop it?"

"There's nothing I can do or you can do for that matter. They are not our problem. If you interfere you will end up dead. That is the real world in which we live. It is the world I grew up in. My mother's sister married an important man, what in the films they would call a gangster. When my father was killed, I was only fifteen and we had no money so I went to my uncle and asked him if I could work for him in some capacity. My mother was too proud to ask and didn't like him but he was always okay to me. I didn't know then he was a gangster or what he was truly like. He looked at me and asked if I was a virgin. I said I was and he offered me five hundred euros to have sex with him. I snapped off his hand for the money and he took me immediately, bent over his desk. That was my introduction to men."

"I'm sorry," was all Afina could think to say. There had been times when they had been so short of money at home she might have considered a similar offer, five hundred euros was an enormous sum.

"A little later he asked me if I wanted to work for him, having sex with his important clients. I was sixteen at the time. Soon I was doing parties with multiple men but he paid me less and less. He had videos and threatened to show them to my mother and the rest of the world if I didn't comply." Mara took a drink of her coffee and raised her eyebrows in an air of resignation. "What could I do?"

Afina was shocked by Mara's revelations. "How did you come to be in England?" she asked.

"Stefan knew what his father was putting me through and he felt sorry for me. He had been my big cousin growing up and I guess he considered me a bit like the younger sister he never had. He asked me if I wanted to come to England to work and I jumped at the chance to make some real money doing what I was good at. I didn't think his father would allow it but he spoke to his father and somehow convinced him I would be useful in England. So here I am."

Afina now understood that Mara felt she owed Stefan for his getting her to England and though she might not approve of his business, she wasn't going to take up sides against him.

"Our lives have many similarities," Afina said. "But why do you stay?"

"What would you have me do? Go back home to my uncle?"

"You can't do this for ever."

"When I have more money perhaps I will start my own business and live off other girls doing the fucking for a change."

There was a knock at the door before Afina could respond. Mara answered and stepped back, surprised to see Victor.

"Hello Mara," Victor said. "I need to speak with Afina."

Afina involuntarily took a couple of spaces further back into the room. She didn't want to speak with Victor.

"What about, Victor?" Mara asked.

"It is not your business," Victor said sharply. "Afina, let's go up to your room."

Mara was blocking the door but Victor pushed past. "I haven't all day, Afina. Let's go."

"There are some new girls," Mara said. "Do you want me to beat one of them for you?"

"I need to speak with Afina privately. I am not looking for my normal entertainment. Perhaps after I speak with Afina."

Afina was worried but a little happier to hear Victor did not seem to want to beat her again. But what did he want to discuss? She knew she had no option but to do as he said so she led the way back up to her room.

As she entered the lounge Stefan was not to be seen.

"Let's go in your bedroom for privacy," Victor suggested. "I have a message from Dimitry for your ears only."

Afina did as instructed and nervously led the way to her bedroom. Victor closed the door. Afina said nothing and waited for Victor to speak.

"Stefan says I must be careful not to damage you because you are earning us a load of money." Victor approached Afina and as he touched her face she instinctively recoiled.

"What do you want?" Afina asked trying to keep her voice steady.

"I have a deal I wish to put to you. If you tell me where you have written this diary of events you have hidden, you will be able to continue working here with no change to the arrangement you have made with Stefan. It is a generous offer."

Afina was terrified. "The diary is my insurance."

"Afina, you are going to tell me everything I want to know. The only question is how much pain you are going to endure first."

Afina was frozen to the spot. She had nowhere she could run and nobody was going to come to her rescue. She knew her limits. She had previously received twenty strokes of the cane from Victor and she had no doubt there was a number of strokes at which she would be prepared to say anything to get him to stop. Then she would be putting the lives of Emma and Becky in danger.

There was only one other option. "I have written two letters and left them with a friend," she admitted. "I can go and get them and bring them back to you."

"We can go and get them together," Victor stated. "You are not leaving my sight until I get these letters."

Afina had expected as much. She also believed there was a high probability Victor would abuse or even kill her after he had what he wanted. "The letters are sealed so my friend doesn't know what they say. I can just quietly ask for them back."

"Who is this friend and where does he live?"

Afina was trying to think fast. "His name is Powell. He lives about ten minutes away. He helped me the night I ran away from here and took me back to his place. He doesn't know anything about what happened. I told him I was running away from an abusive boyfriend when he found me on the street."

"Are you fucking him?"

"Don't be mad. He's old enough to be my father. He was nice to me so I asked him to keep the letters for me."

"Does he know what's in them?"

"No, I just said they were some important personal papers and I would collect them when I was settled."

She realised she was potentially putting Powell in danger but she really had no other option. At least Victor had never met or heard of Powell. She almost said his name was Danny but was worried Victor would mention the name to Stefan before they left and that would create too many complications.

"So let's go visit this Powell. Call him to let him know you are coming."

Afina picked up her mobile from the table and called the number listed as Danny. She was praying Victor didn't look closely at her phone and see she was calling someone called Danny.

"It's Afina," she said when Powell answered. "Can I come and see you? I'd like to take back the two letters I left with you. I want to update them."

There was a brief silence at the other end of the line while Powell digested Afina's surprising request. He was aware someone could be listening to her call.

"Of course," Powell replied. "When do you want to come?"

"How about right now?"

"Okay. Do you remember where I live?"

"I remember the name of the bar."

"I'll expect you in about ten minutes."

Afina ended the call and put the phone in her pocket. "He expects us in ten minutes."

"Good," Victor said simply. "We can take a taxi."

CHAPTER TWENTY FOUR

Powell had ten minutes to prepare for the arrival of Afina and almost certainly she would not be coming alone. Afina had told him about the letters she had left with her friends. Someone, could it possibly even be Dimitry, was threatening her in order to recover the letters. Powell hoped Afina hadn't been hurt. She had sounded nervous but otherwise okay on the telephone. At least she had had the good sense to tell whoever was threatening her that he had the letters. If she had given up the names of the girls there was no way of knowing what might have happened. They could have all ended up dead.

Powell went to his desk in the office behind the bar and filled two envelopes with blank pages. Then he placed them inside his safe. He was going to have to be careful when Afina arrived. There were various scenarios playing out in his head but whether it was Stefan or someone else about to pay a visit, he didn't see how he could let them ever leave, as they would quickly discover the envelopes were empty and then Afina would be in grave danger.

Stefan turning up would be the worst possible result as he was the only person who knew him as Danny and he very much wanted to keep both his alter ego and relationship with Stefan in play. Stefan still offered the best possible chance to find Dimitry.

The bar was relatively quiet being early evening and Powell poured himself a shot of whisky, which he downed in one, then he informed the two guys working the bar he was expecting visitors and he would be in his office. He had CCTV covering the entrance and interior of the bar so he would be able to spot Afina entering and possible identify who she was with, if she didn't come alone. He sat watching the feed from the cameras, which was more normally used to spot drunks causing trouble. He planned to meet whoever arrived in the bar itself, as he assumed the presence of people scattered around the bar would deter whoever was with Afina from getting too violent in public.

Powell saw the taxi pull up out front and while happy not to see any sign of Stefan, he was disappointed it was a stranger and not Dimitry who accompanied Afina towards the entrance to the bar. She entered, looked around and then she spotted Powell walking towards her. He gave a cheerful wave of recognition.

"Hi Afina," Powell welcomed her with a kiss on each cheek. "Who's your friend?"

"This is Victor."

"Hello Victor, I'm Powell." They shook hands briefly. "Can I get you both a drink?"

"No thank you," Victor replied. "We are in a hurry."

"Well the letters are in the office. Come through and I'll get them for you."

Powell was relieved when Victor and then Afina, followed him towards the office. He had been worried Victor would just expect him to fetch the letters by himself and hand them over in the bar. Powell held the office door open for them both and then closed it behind them. He went to the safe, which was sat on the floor in one corner. He entered the combination and the door swung open. He reached inside and withdrew the envelopes, holding them out in one hand to Afina for her to take. She approached and as she took them in her hand, he withdrew his other hand from the safe and it now contained a pistol aimed at Victor.

"What the fuck," Victor reacted to the site of the weapon.

"Sit down, Victor," Powell instructed, pointing towards the sole chair positioned behind the desk.

Victor didn't move at first. "You are both going to regret this," he threatened. "Especially you Afina. I'm going to enjoy giving you one hundred strokes of my cane. Do you have any idea what…?"

"Shut the fuck up, Victor and sit down," Powell interrupted. He waved the gun towards the chair.

Afina was hanging back behind Powell. "What do we do next?" she asked. She had been as shocked as Victor to see the gun in Powell's hand.

"Ten minutes isn't much time to come up with a plan." Powell replied. "You did the right thing bringing him here though."

"Stefan will be expecting us back," Afina said, obviously worried.

"You are both dead," Victor laughed. "You can't hold me here for ever. And if you run I will find you."

"I think you're probably right, Victor. So you don't leave me with much choice."

"You aren't going to shoot me," Victor said confidently. "Shooting someone is much easier in the movies than real life."

"That's true but I've shot more than my share of people in the past."

Victor looked surprised by Powell's revelation. "You were in the army?" he asked.

"Let's just say I worked for the government."

Victor started to look uncomfortable.

"Victor is good friends with Dimitry," Afina interjected.

"Is that so?" Powell asked.

"I have known Dimitry a long time. Yes, we are friends."

"Did you see the name of this bar when you entered?" Powell asked.

"The name. No I didn't see the bloody name."

"It's called Bella's after my daughter. She was a young police officer out one night with a colleague when she came across your friend."

It took Victor a few seconds to understand what he was hearing then all the blood drained from his face. "I had nothing to do with what happened to your daughter. It was that stupid bitch's fault." He pointed accusingly at Afina.

"No Victor, it wasn't Afina's fault. She wasn't the one organising human trafficking. I hold Dimitry, Stefan and now you, responsible for my daughter's death, so understand I will have no compunction about shooting you if necessary."

"It was nothing to do with me. I would not be so stupid as to kill a police officer."

"Perhaps not but you are still guilty by association. Now put your phone on the floor and slide it towards me," Powell instructed.

Victor silently did as asked. His eyes were fixed on Afina.

"What are you looking at?" Afina asked, becoming unnerved by Victor's stare."

"Don't let him get to you," Powell cautioned. "He won't ever hurt you again."

Powell checked the contacts in Victor's phone and satisfied it contained a number for Dimitry, he put the phone inside his back pocket. He wasn't sure what to do with Victor but knew he had to make him disappear. Killing him in cold blood wasn't an option. It had been a long time since he would consider such an action even remotely morally acceptable.

He could think of only one short term solution. The bar had a secure basement and an even securer cellar area within the basement, where the expensive champagnes and vintage spirits were kept permanently locked. It was known to the staff as Aladdin's cave.

"We are going downstairs," Powell announced. "If you behave yourself, your life is not in imminent danger but if you try to make a run for it, I will be left with no option but to shoot you."

Victor offered no response other than a glare. He didn't look happy but realised he had few options.

Powell made Victor walk ahead of him as they left the office, turned a corner and took the steps down to the basement. They were hidden from the view of customers but not staff so Powell was happy they didn't bump into anyone, it might prove difficult to answer questions about why the owner was wielding a gun.

Once down the stairs, Powell pushed Victor towards one end of the basement where the cage like feature protected the valuable drinks. He removed the key from his pocket and kept his distance from Victor as he ushered him inside.

"I shall be just upstairs and if I hear any noise from you I will have to take steps to silence you," Powell warned. "I'll even feed you later if you behave yourself."

"You can't keep me here for ever," Victor warned.

"True but if I was you I'd behave as the minute you start making a nuisance of yourself, I will start rethinking whether you are worth keeping alive."

Returning upstairs Powell locked the basement door. He went and found Neil and told him the basement was out of use for the rest of the evening. He looked surprised but knew trips to the expensive cellar were relatively rare so it was only a small inconvenience at worst.

Powell took Afina back to his office. "Afina, you can't go back to Stefan. I am going to have to make Victor disappear for some time and Stefan knows you left with Victor, so if you go back alone he will be deeply suspicious. It's too dangerous."

"What will you do with Victor?"

"I'm not sure. At some point he has to be set free and he is then going to be like a wounded Bull looking for revenge against all of us. I don't have the answer at the moment."

"If I'm not to go back, where can I stay?"

"I have an apartment upstairs you can use."

"I'm not sure."

"It will be your own apartment. I have a house nearby where I stay. The apartment was Bella's place for the last couple of years and it's probably a bit of a mess."

"I don't have much money."

"If you want a job we always need waitresses and bar staff."

Afina smiled broadly, "I came to England to work in a bar, now I have a proper job at last."

"I think it best you don't go out much for the time being. I need to decide what to do with Victor and tomorrow I'm going to see Stefan and push him for me to meet his contact in Romania. I'm hoping that will be Dimitry."

"What about my mama and Adriana? When I don't go back they will be in danger."

"Can they go stay with some family temporarily?"

"I have an aunt but her apartment is not very big. They can't stay long."

"I just need to buy some time while I decide what we do next. Would your mother and sister like to visit England perhaps? There is enough room upstairs for them."

"Mama doesn't speak English. And what reason am I going to give her for having to leave?"

"The truth. You witnessed a murder and though you are safe, you're worried for them."

"I will call mama and see what she says."

CHAPTER TWENTY FIVE

Powell called Stefan and informed him he had transferred the fifty thousand pounds. He then asked to see Afina. Not surprisingly, Stefan said she was unavailable as she had gone away for a few days. Stefan suggested he see Mara and Powell said he would if Afina didn't return within a few days. Powell then arranged to meet Stefan a couple of hours later.

"Afina didn't mention she was going away," Powell said, when he arrived at Stefan's.

"It was a sudden decision. Her mother was taken ill."

Powell smiled inwardly because he knew Afina's mother was perfectly well and on an aeroplane to England. "I have been speaking with my investors and they feel I should make a trip to Romania to meet your contacts out there. After all, we have now given you a lot of money and if something was to happen to you, I would have no idea who to speak to or anything."

"That makes sense. When were you thinking of going?"

"Sooner the better really. I have nothing stopping me being on a plane tomorrow. Would you come with me or should I just meet someone over there?"

"I can't really get away at the moment but I can arrange for my business partner to meet you and show you around a little, answer your questions and maybe introduce you to some of our nice Romanian girls."

"That would be great." At the mention of meeting Stefan's business partner, Powell was very hopeful it would be Dimitry.

"There is a flight from Gatwick tomorrow afternoon with Easyjet, which I sometimes take when I want a weekend back home. It arrives about nine in the evening so I can arrange for you to be met and taken to a nice hotel. Then my partner can pick you up about ten thirty and show you our night life."

"Sounds good. I'll book the flight and text you to confirm when it's done. What's your partner's name?"

"Victor."

Powell was a little taken aback by the name he least expected to hear. Victor was still in the cage back at the bar nursing a very bad hangover. Powell had taken him some food the previous evening and found him three quarters of the way through an expensive bottle of brandy. Victor's sorrows were well and truly drowned. Powell had thought it a small price to pay for the lack of trouble he was getting from Victor. Even so, he knew he couldn't keep him locked up in his basement for much longer. He had threatened him that if he drank more than one bottle per day he would break every finger on one hand the first time he did it and if he did it again he wouldn't be lifting any glass unaided for a very long time.

Powell doubted Stefan had two close associates called Victor so he wasn't sure how to interpret Stefan's choice of name. Perhaps it was Dimitry but Stefan thought it safer to use a different name. Anyway, in thirty six hours he would know the answer.

"Stefan, I think I am going to enjoy working with you. You seem to know how to look after your business partners, plenty of girls and some fun alongside the business. Definitely a recipe for success!"

"Are you sure you wouldn't like to see Mara? She is free right now and it would be on the house."

"Not this time. I'd better get back and book my ticket. Next week if Afina isn't back, then I'll be paying Mara a visit."

"Good. I will call Victor and organise your visit."

Once back at the bar Powell booked the flight and then a quick check on Victor revealed he was feeling better after a late brunch and plenty of coffee. Powell had given him a couple of newspapers to read and told him he would be allowed to leave the next day. Victor looked a bit dubious but Powell had lied, telling him he had only been holding onto him long enough for Afina and her family to escape the country. In truth, Powell had to move him before the staff asked any more awkward questions. He was also getting fed up of managing the regular visits to the bathroom, which were required as he didn't fancy a mess in his cellar.

Powell bundled Afina into his car and headed for Gatwick to collect her mother and sister. He didn't like leaving Victor unattended but Afina had begged him to accompany her to Gatwick. The round trip would be less than two hours and with Victor locked in the drinks cellar, inside the locked basement, he thought everything should be okay.

The plane was on time and Powell enjoyed seeing the family reunion as

Afina greeted her mother and sister. It was a warm moment in what had otherwise been a very bleak couple of weeks. Afina introduced Powell in obviously glowing terms. Though he couldn't understand a word that was said, the crushing embrace from Afina's mother and the look in her eyes said everything.

Once back at the bar, Powell left the family to settle in to the upstairs apartment. He had finally decided what to do with Victor. It would involve asking Brian for an enormous favour but they had done something similar in their younger days. Of course, that had been sanctioned by the government and this was a completely different situation but Brian owed him and it was time to collect.

Brian answered immediately and brief pleasantries out of the way, Powell came straight to the point. "I need your help with something important."

"It sounds serious. What do you need?"

"Remember Jimmy Govern?"

"That scumbag enforcer we had put away for self-harming? Of course I do, it was one of our cleverer ideas."

"I need something similar."

"Powell, you have to be joking."

"I'm deadly serious. Right now I have someone locked in my basement who isn't dissimilar to Govern. I need him held out of the way for at least two weeks."

"Powell, these are different times. Who is this guy?"

"He's a very nasty Romanian gangster. If I let him go we'll never find Dimitry."

There was silence for a few seconds at the other end of the phone.

"Okay," Brian finally said. "We have a secure unit near Portsmouth. If we have him admitted for attempted suicide with an ongoing risk of self-harm, we can probably keep him locked up in isolation for at least a couple of weeks. Like with Jimmy Govern, he needs to be delivered sedated and pretty much out of it. When we eventually let him go he'll have a medical history that says he attempted suicide and is delusional. He will also have a warning that should he make any wild claims, it will be taken as further proof of his delusional behaviour and he'll be locked up again."

"I owe you for this, Brian."

"Please don't ask for anything else. I'll send a car to collect him. Say about eight tonight?"

"Perfect. I'll have him ready and compliable. His name is Victor but I don't know his surname. If you run a check on him it's possible he'll be wanted for crimes either here or back home."

"I'll have him checked out. We need to talk soon about what you're up to."

"Agreed but I'm out of the country for a few days. We'll talk when I get back."

"Romania by any chance?"

"I'm following a lead which I hope will take me to Dimitry. Actually I need one further favour. "

"Blimey, Powell. It might be a good thing you haven't been around the last twenty years, I have a feeling I might not have had such a glittering career, continually helping you out. Go on, what do you need?"

Powell proceeded to explain the assistance he was going to need.

"Good luck and keep in touch," Brian said, after agreeing to provide Powell with what he needed and hastily ending the call before his friend came up with any further requests, which would put his pension at risk.

Running a popular bar in the Brighton area meant Powell had more than once had to keep a close eye on someone he thought might be dealing in drugs and evicted them from the premises. He didn't want Bella brought up around drugs or his bar getting a reputation as a place where drugs were easily available. However, he did know one person he had suspicions about but had never actually seen him sell anything. His name was Scott something and Powell knew he was known to a couple of the bar staff. He was lucky that Dave, who worked behind the bar most nights had his phone number. A quick phone call and an arrangement was made.

Powell collected what he wanted two hours later. Scott hadn't had what he specifically wanted but had known where to get some. Powell returned with his purchase and included a liberal amount in some coffee he took down to Victor along with a sandwich.

It took only thirty minutes for the sedative to take effect and he knew the effects would last for about four or five hours. Victor was acting not much differently to the previous night when he was blind drunk but this time he hadn't had any alcohol. He was unsteady on his feet and Powell had to help support him, which meant putting his weapon away in his jacket. Fortunately, Victor was in such a state he obligingly staggered out to the waiting car just on the promise he was going home. Two men jumped out the car and helped Powell bundle Victor in the back seat, where he immediately laid down. A minute later the car was speeding away and Powell hurried back inside to plan with Afina what they were going to do next.

The thought of Victor waking up to find himself in a secure hospital made Powell smile broadly. Victor would probably not make a great patient. In fact, he'd be screaming blue murder once he was conscious but it wouldn't do him any good. If he made too much noise they would simply sedate him again.

CHAPTER TWENTY SIX

Powell had given Afina strict instructions not to go out and certainly not allow her mother or Adriana out until he returned. They had a natural curiosity to visit the town but Powell had been firm, it was too dangerous. He would be away for just the weekend and they could stay inside. He promised he would then take them to London sightseeing as soon as it was safe.

The flight was uneventful and he showed the passport describing him as Danny Jones, a relic of time spent undercover more than twenty years ago when a second identity had been a necessity. He was glad he'd renewed the passport despite no obvious need for it over the last few years. As he emerged from customs at Bucharest airport, he saw the man waiting for him holding the sign saying Danny. Powell knew immediately it wasn't Dimitry. This man was rounder than he was tall and waddled rather than walked. Powell immediately assumed he was just a driver sent to collect him and take him to his hotel. Dimitry wouldn't take the risk of coming in person and possibly being identified by a vigilant local policeman.

As it turned out, Powell was correct in his assessment and the man he was due to meet, who went by the name of Victor, had indeed arranged for him to be collected and taken to a hotel in the city centre, with the deserving name of Grand Hotel. Deserving because the hotel was truly luxurious and adorned with antiques and beautiful works of art that wouldn't look out of place in a Palace. It certainly wasn't the type of hotel Powell regularly frequented.

Powell had been told by the driver to be in reception at ten thirty and was duly waiting downstairs when in walked a further stranger.

"Danny?" the stranger asked.

"That's me." Powell hid his disappointment that this man wasn't Dimitry.

"I am Bogdan. Come with me."

Obviously a man of few words. Powell followed the man outside to a large, shiny looking Mercedes and began to reassess whether his first assessment this was a grunt not someone more important was correct. They drove for about ten minutes without conversation and pulled into a side street in an old part of town. There had been a large number of busy bars and clubs on the main road, which suggested it could be the centre of Bucharest's nightlife.

The driver led the way, striding out quickly without saying anything further, obviously expecting Powell to follow. He turned back onto the main road, which was a wide Boulevard busy with people despite the late hour and after a short distance they arrived at a café come bar. Powell followed the man inside, who nodded in recognition at a large man blocking the top of some stairs leading downwards and he stood aside, letting them pass. At the bottom of the stairs was a small and intimate club with a dance floor area, where two attractive young girls were doing a strip show. Other girls were performing lap dances for customers in small booths. Music was playing and there was a bar running down one side of the room.

A group of three men were sitting in a semi-circular booth around a table containing drinks. They looked up as Powell approached. He had no doubt the man in the middle was Dimitry and he felt an immediate, immense desire to take him by the throat and crush the life from him. This was the man who stabbed Bella and ended her life just when it should have been beginning. Powell fought with his emotions not wishing to reveal his true feelings and contented himself with the thought that now he had found Dimitry, he would soon claim justice for her death. The problem was that wasn't actually enough to bring him much comfort, nothing would ever heal the feeling of loss.

"You must be Danny," Dimitry said with a welcoming smile.

"Are you Victor?" Powell asked.

"No, I am Dimitry. Victor couldn't be here but don't worry I am also the business partner of Victor and Stefan."

"Nice place you have here," Powell said, sitting beside Dimitry as space was made for him.

"Not bad," Dimitry agreed. "Would you like a drink?"

"A beer would be good."

"We can't drink beer!" Dimitry raised his hand and immediately a girl appeared to take their order. "A bottle of the good champagne and a bottle of Tuica."

"So Danny, you are our new business partner. We will find you some good girls. It shouldn't be too difficult, we have many nice girls in Romania who want to travel to England. We will find you some to try out before you leave."

"I'm sure Stefan has told you I have specific requirements."

"Not a problem, you want girls like Afina when she first arrived in England. Stefan tells me you have been fucking her."

"Yes I like Afina. I guess when she first came to England she was the type of young rather innocent girl I am looking for. She is not so innocent now."

"That is partly my fault. I had to teach her what it is to be fucked by a real man not some boy."

The drinks arrived and the waitress poured a glass of champagne and a shot of the Tuica.

"Tuica is a bit like vodka," Dimitry explained. "But made from plums, stronger and is our national drink." He raised his glass in a toast, "To new partners."

Powell noticed the others all downed the shot in one so he did likewise. Owning a bar for ten years he had tried most drinks but this really burned and made him wince. "That certainly has a kick," he confirmed.

Dimitry laughed and refilled the glasses. He raised his glass in a further toast, "To girls."

Once again Powell downed the drink in one. "My turn for a toast," he said, as the glasses were refilled. "Here's to a long life and a merry one, a quick death and an easy one, a pretty girl and a true one, a drink called Tuica and another one." The third drink tasted a great deal smoother than the first one.

"A great toast, Danny. I can see you like our drink."

"I do but I'll stick to champagne now, if you don't mind, otherwise you'll be carrying me out of here."

Dimitry raised his hand and waved at a couple of girls standing at the bar. "This is Danny," he said when they walked over. "He is visiting us for the first time. Take him in a booth and give him one of our special private dances."

One of the girls held out her hand and Powell took hold of it and followed the two girls to a booth with a curtain in front. He felt it would have been rude to refuse Dimitry's hospitality. Once behind the curtain he was seated and the girls started seductively dancing in front of him as they removed their clothes. One was blonde and the other brunette. Both were beautiful and it was no hardship to watch them or let them start to give him a very intimate lap dance. One of the girls had her breasts in his face and he couldn't see what the other was doing but he felt his belt undone and her pulling on the zip to his jeans.

"Hold on," he said, pulling his zip back up and sitting up straighter in the chair. "The dance is enough, thank you."

The girls looked concerned. "Don't you like us?" the blonde asked in good English.

"I think you're both amazing but a dance is enough," he reiterated.

"But Dimitry said to give you the special private dance. That means a blowjob as well."

"And I'm sure you both give great blowjobs but I'm not in the mood. Don't worry, I'll tell Dimitry you were both excellent."

The girls seemed happier and relaxed. "I'm Daniela," the blonde introduced herself. "And this is Nicola."

Both girls kissed him on the cheek, which Powell found faintly amusing as they were both completely naked and only just introducing themselves.

"Can I get you girls a drink?" Powell asked.

"Not sure," Daniela answered. "Ask Dimitry. He owns the place and we work for him. We can join you at your table if he wants."

"I'll do exactly that," Powell answered and strode back to the table where Dimitry was sitting.

"You were quick," Dimitry laughed.

"Can the girls join us?" Powell asked.

"Sure." He beckoned to the girls to come over. "Get some more glasses and another bottle of champagne."

"Thank you, Dimitry. You have a great club. And of course, great girls!"

"What did I tell you? We have beautiful girls in Romania."

The girls returned carrying champagne and glasses. They squeezed either side of Powell.

"I have to be going now," Dimitry announced. "The girls are my gift for the evening so enjoy them and the drinks are on me. Order some more champagne or whatever you wish. I think you may have a sore head in the morning so I will see you in reception at eleven."

Powell shook hands and watched Dimitry and his friends leave. As he sat back down the girls were both smiling excitedly.

"You must be important," Nicola said.

"Not really."

"Dimitry just gave you both of us for the night. Do you know how much that costs?" Daniela asked.

"No doubt a huge amount of money but for now let's try and drink as much of his expensive champagne as possible."

The two Englishmen at the nearby table had been getting louder the more they drank and were suddenly shouting at the girl who had brought them their bill, complaining they had been overcharged. They both had south London accents.

"I know we're tourists but we're not bloody stupid," the older of the two men was saying in a decidedly slurred manner, testimony to the amount he had drunk.

"Sir, the bill lists everything you drank."

"It's not the number of drinks I'm disputing, it's the bloody price of the drinks. Three hundred pounds for a cheap bottle of champagne is ridiculous."

"The price includes the entertainment."

"Well we're not paying," the younger man said, who had so far remained silent. "It's taking the piss to call what you offer, entertainment! I've seen better in my local pub."

Powell noticed the girl look in the direction of the bar in an obvious request for some help. The man behind the bar picked up his phone and said something brief.

One minute later two large men, obviously the equivalent of English bouncers, walked down the stairs and towards the two men.

"Time to pay your bill and be on your way," the first bouncer, who had a goatee beard said, in surprisingly good English. "We don't want any trouble."

"Trouble, don't take the piss you oversized fairy. Get the fuck out of here," the older drunk replied.

"You have ten seconds to provide a credit card to pay your bill or you are going to wake up in hospital," goatee threatened.

"Okay, okay," the older drunk said, staggering to his feet. "No need to get nasty." He reached into his inside pocket to withdraw his wallet but instead there was suddenly a gun in his hand.

Both the bouncers took a quick backward step. The second drunk suddenly seemed much more sober as he also took a gun from inside his jacket.

"So now who is going to end up in hospital tomorrow?" the younger drunk asked.

The unarmed bouncers looked worried. "Just leave," the goatee said.

"What, without paying our bill?" the older drunk asked with heavy sarcasm. "What sort of people do you think we are?"

The young drunk seemed to notice Powell for the first time. "How come you get two beautiful ladies?" he asked. He addressed the girls, "Why don't you come and sit with us and we'll order some more champagne."

"They're with me," Powell said simply.

"You English?" the older drunk asked.

"Yes."

"If you know what's good for you, I'd get out of here," the older drunk threatened, waving his gun at Powell.

"I think you're probably right. I have an early start in the morning." Powell stood up. "It's been fun," he said to the girls and made to leave.

"They're all yours," Powell said to the drunks as he came level.

He moved so fast it was over before anyone understood it had started. He grabbed the wrist of the young drunk, who happened to be nearest, and twisted, at the same time forcing the man's arm back in a move that made it easy to ease the gun from the man's hand. He released the man's arm, pushing him aside in the same instant and kicking his legs away so he fell to the floor. Before anyone knew what had happened, Powell was suddenly pointing the gun at the older drunk, who had a look of disbelief on his face.

"Drop the gun," Powell ordered calmly.

The man was indecisive for about five seconds and then placed his gun on the table in front of him. "Look, we were just having a bit of fun," he said. "We weren't really going to hurt anyone."

"You should be careful where you choose to play with those things," Powell warned. "I could have simply shot you when I disarmed your jerk friend."

The second drunk was lying on the floor, watching proceedings. He managed to get up by holding on to a chair.

"Now give the nice girl your credit card and you can be on your way," Powell said. The older drunk hurriedly withdrew his wallet and handed a card to the waitress.

"They're just drunk," Powell said to the two bouncers, who looked ready to cause trouble. "I apologise on behalf of my countrymen. They probably drank too much of your Tuica." He gave his friendliest smile. "That stuff's got a real kick!"

The girl took only a minute to insert the credit card in the machine she had been holding and then she handed it to the man to enter his pin number. "I added a generous tip," she said with a smile.

The man grudgingly entered his number and returned the machine to the waitress.

Once the girl had returned the credit card receipt, Powell said, "Let's go," indicating the stairs.

The bouncers stood back and Powell followed the drunks upstairs. He lowered the gun and put it in his trouser pocket to avoid attention from the other customers.

There were a couple of taxis waiting outside for business. The two men climbed into the first even as Powell was saying, "I'd get as far away from here as possible and don't come back."

He headed back downstairs and passed the two bouncers on the stairs. "Thank you for your help. I'm sure the boss will be very grateful," goatee said.

"If you mean Dimitry, we are business partners in England so it was nothing. I was just helping a friend."

"Thank you. If you need anything, please don't hesitate to ask."

"Thanks." Powell shook the offered hand and that of the other bouncer, then headed back to his table.

The girls were excitedly laughing when Powell sat down. "Sorry about the interruption," he said. "What's so funny?"

"The look on the face of the Englishman when you took the gun from his friend," Daniela explained.

Powell reckoned the girls were also laughing out of a sense of relief they were no longer in any danger. "I think we need more champagne," he said.

They spent another hour drinking champagne and appearing to get progressively merrier. At least that was how it would appear to anyone watching. However, he spent far more time filling the glasses of the girls with champagne rather than his own. Fortunately they seemed to have an unlimited capacity for consuming drink so several bottles were delivered to the table.

Powell imagined that someone left in the club would be watching him and giving a report to Dimitry, so he appeared drunker than he actually was and for most of the evening he kept up the pretence of wanting a threesum with both girls. It was an enjoyable evening and both girls gave him further very hot lap dances.

About one thirty he was feeling tired. "I need to get some sleep tonight," Powell said. "And I fear if I take you back to my hotel room I won't be getting any sleep so I'm going to call it a night and head back alone." The idea of spending further time with them was very attractive but ultimately they were tainted by their association with Dimitry.

"But we won't get paid if you don't sleep with us," Nicola complained.

Powell had forgotten they were with him to make money not any other reason. So they left together and took a taxi back to his hotel where he put them in further taxis back to where they lived. They had all agreed in the taxi to say they spent the night together but Powell had been very tired and fallen asleep after some very quick sex.

Powell went up to his room, inserted the card key and entered. He almost jumped out of his skin, when the two drunks from the club stepped out from behind the bathroom door.

"Christ," Powell swore. "Where'd you two come from."

"Sorry," the older drunk said, now quite sober. "We were just hiding in case it was someone other than you."

"Great job, guys," Powell said. "That should cement my relationship with Dimitry. Give my thanks to Brian."

"Our pleasure. Will you be needing anything else?" the older drunk asked.

"No, that's more than enough, thanks. You better make yourselves scarce. I wouldn't want you bumping into Dimitry or any of his crowd."

"In that case, if you're sure we're not needed, we'll be on the first plane back to England. Good luck with whatever it is you're doing."

"Thanks," Powell said, shaking hands. "Enjoy your flight."

Powell went to sleep a happy man. He had found Bella's killer and so far the plan was working. He didn't yet know exactly how he was going to get Dimitry back to England, which was still his ultimate aim, so he could be arrested and tried but he was confident he would find a way. He hoped the night's events in the club would earn Dimitry's complete trust, which in turn would afford him the opportunity to manipulate him into returning.

Powell had decided he didn't want to involve the local Romanian police because he didn't understand or trust the local legal system. If they put

Dimitry on bail, he would undoubtedly disappear, perhaps never to be seen again.

His only fall-back plan if everything else went wrong was to eliminate Dimitry but that came with potentially significant risks to himself and ultimately also to Afina and her family, who he now felt a huge responsibility to protect.

CHAPTER TWENTY SEVEN

Powell was in the hotel reception waiting for Dimitry at eleven. After a few minutes Bogdan appeared and once again led him out to the Mercedes. Dimitry was sitting in the back and there was a man Powell recognised from the previous evening sitting in the front.

"I hear you had an exciting evening," Dimitry said, as Powell joined him in the back seat of the car.

"I guess you're not just referring to the girls?" Powell asked with a smile.

"I heard some of your countrymen were causing trouble and you dealt with it very well."

"Least I could do to help, considering how much of your champagne I was drinking."

"Thank you, Danny. I am indebted to you."

"My pleasure. So what's the plan for this morning?"

"We take you to meet some girls we are planning to send to England in the near future. You can tell us if you think they are suitable. We will tell them you help us find the jobs in England."

Powell was overcome with a terrible sense of foreboding. How could he meet these girls and not warn them they must not consider going to England. He wanted justice for Bella but she would never forgive him if he allowed other girls to be put in harm's way in search of that justice. The fact he was even considering that option meant he was losing sight of what made Bella special. He could not put revenge and any personal satisfaction that might provide above what he knew would be Bella's wishes. First and foremost he had to do what she had done, protect the innocent from Dimitry's evil.

"Is it possible for me to have these girls if I like them?" Powell asked.

"Of course. We have just the two to meet today but if you like them I can have them in England for you in just a few days."

"Sounds good."

Powell decided the best way to protect these girls was to say he wanted them. When they arrived in England, he had no further money to complete the purchase of the girls so his rough plan was to have the police intervene during the sale. He could wear a wire and hoped to get enough evidence to have Stefan convicted. Fortunately, both Stefan and Dimitry seemed to trust him, which he was sure was in no small part to his having given them fifty thousand pounds as a deposit for the girls, money he never expected to see again no matter what happened.

Powell was surprised to see they headed back to the café bar where they had met the previous evening. The downstairs was shut but upstairs was busy with people drinking coffee and eating cakes. There was no sign of the bouncers, who presumably weren't on duty during the day. Dimitry joined Powell at a table in one corner while the other guys made themselves scarce.

"Would you like a Tuica?" Dimitry asked with a hint of a smile.

"No thanks, coffee will be fine for now."

Dimitry waved at the girl behind the counter who came and took their order.

"I told the girls to come at twelve, which is about ten minutes. Tell me, what did you think of Nicola and Daniela last night? I hope you took full advantage."

"They are great girls," Powell agreed.

"So tell me more, what did you do with them?"

"Dimitry, I'm English! We don't kiss and tell. It isn't polite"

"Polite! You English are funny. Do you have to politely ask your girlfriend if you can fuck her in the arse? It is different here. We take what we want from our women."

"I think that approach stopped working about a hundred years ago. And maybe it's a good thing. It means men are willing to pay for action they can't get at home."

"True," Dimitry agreed. "And what is it about you English and animals? You care as much for your dogs as your children."

"Well I have neither."

"I only use dogs to protect what is mine and I don't have any children, at least not that I know of," Dimitry laughed out loud, causing heads to turn in their direction.

"So Dimitry, when are you coming to England?" Powell asked. "Can you come next week with the girls?"

"England is a little difficult for me at the moment."

"Really? That is a nuisance because I am sure my investors would like to meet you and I would like the opportunity to return your hospitality. If we are to do more business it is necessary for my investors to meet with all key people. I can also promise you it would be a lot of fun. They know how to party. We would organise something very special for you with some of our English girls."

"It may be possible. You say your friends like to party? Well I like to party and actually a friend of mine has gone missing in Brighton recently so I should make a visit and try to find out what has happened to him."

"Perhaps I can be of service? I have many contacts."

"Thank you Danny. Your help would be much appreciated."

Afina called Emma and Becky to ask them if they would like to come for a drink as it was Saturday evening and for once she was free to meet with them on a Saturday. Powell had said she couldn't leave the bar but inviting her friends over for a few cocktails would be fun.

"We've never been here before," Becky said when they arrived. "It's a nice place. Is this where you work?"

"Yes but I am not working tonight."

"Good, can we get cheap drinks?" Emma asked.

Powell had said to Neil that anything Afina wanted should be put on his tab. "Drinks are on me all night," she confirmed.

"Brilliant, I hope they stay open late," Emma joked.

"Pity it's a straight bar," Becky laughed.

"So, what shall we drink?" Afina asked. "White wine?"

"Great," both girls answered in unison.

Afina went to the bar and the girls sat at a table. Afina went white when she turned back from the bar with the opened bottle of wine and glasses, to find Mara sat talking to the girls. She approached the table slowly, in a state of shock.

"Hello Mara, what are you doing here?" Afina asked coldly.

"Hi Afina. I just wanted to say hello."

Afina's heart was pumping at a hundred miles an hour. Why was Mara here and how had she found her? Did this mean Stefan was nearby? "Excuse me, Becky and Emma, but I need to speak with Mara alone." Afina walked away from the table and Mara followed.

"How did you find me?" Afina asked, once out of earshot of the others.

"Stefan had me follow you on your last night out. You went to a gay bar with your new friends. I guess you have gone off men since working in England."

"So what did you tell Stefan?"

"Just that you went for drinks in a gay bar. He thought it was hilarious. I didn't mention about your friends."

Afina relaxed a little. "Why are you here tonight?"

"Because Stefan is trying to find you and he told me to visit the bar where I followed you before."

"I don't understand. How did you come here?"

"I spotted your friends at the bar and when they left I wondered if they might be meeting you so I followed them here."

"Why didn't you tell me you followed me before?"

"I didn't want you to know. You are my friend and it wasn't a nice thing to do, spying on you, but I had no choice."

"You promise Stefan doesn't know I am here?"

"I promise. Now let's have some wine. I like the look of your friends. Perhaps they might like a threesum with me."

"Mara! They think I work in this bar. They don't know what I do, did."

"Okay, Okay! I won't tell them if you don't say anything about me."

Afina led the way back to the table where the girls were already drinking the wine. She was worried about the presence of Mara. She was Stefan's cousin and Afina wasn't totally convinced she could be trusted. Then again, she couldn't have told Stefan about Emma and Becky, and where they lived, or Victor would have gone there looking for the letter. Afina was pleased Powell was not around to further complicate matters.

As the evening progressed, Mara proved to be a terrible flirt. Afina watched with a broad smile as Mara admitted she had never had a relationship with a girl but then added she had fucked a load of them, which made everyone laugh. More than once, some men tried to chat to them and offered to buy drinks but each time they were told clearly that everyone at the table was gay, which Afina didn't bother to point out wasn't entirely true.

Afina could see that her friends were both drawn to Mara's outgoing nature and good looks. Afina wondered if Mara had always been into girls or was it a direct result of her work. Afina enjoyed going out with girls but the thought of taking them home to bed at the end of the evening just didn't appeal.

They all consumed a large amount of wine and tequila shots before the discussion turned to where they were going next. Afina was adamant she was going to bed despite everyone else's protestations. She would have quite liked to party a little longer but she had no intention of breaking her promise to Powell and what none of them knew was that her family was asleep upstairs. They were now her first priority and she was not going to leave them alone at the bar, sleeping or not.

Eventually Mara left with the girls, heading for a gay club that stayed open all night. Afina was convinced they were all going to end up in bed together at some point during the night.

CHAPTER TWENTY EIGHT

Powell had told Dimitry he would take both girls they had met in the café. They were young, attractive and excited to work in England. Powell also thought they were amazingly naïve. They asked few detailed questions about the potential job although they did want to know if Brighton was good for shopping and going out. Powell could see how easy it was for Dimitry to find girls. He wondered how many girls had passed through his and Stefan's hands on the way to a life as a sex slave.

Powell had never met anyone quite as callous as Dimitry and his friends. It was almost as if they had been born without feelings, the way they had such a total disregard for the wellbeing of girls and there was a deep rooted lack of respect, as if the girls were just commodities not human beings.

In his past, Powell had dealt with the worst of terrorists from Northern Ireland and though he didn't agree with their politics or methods, he could at least understand their motivation. Then again, he could understand Dimitry's motivation, it was pure greed. Powell wondered what his upbringing had been like to turn him into the adult monster he had become. Some psychologist would probably claim he had been abused as a child and it wasn't his fault. Well that was the sort of bullshit he heard far too often in a society that was too politically correct, always trying to find excuses for bad behaviour. In Powell's experience, some people were just evil and he had unfortunately encountered too many of them in his life. He would put an end to Dimitry, Stefan and Victor's business that preyed on innocent young girls, if it was the last thing he ever accomplished.

Powell had told Dimitry, he wanted to explore the city a little before joining up with him again for dinner at the club. He needed to stretch his legs and breathe in fresh air as he found every minute spent with Dimitry very claustrophobic. The memory of what he had done to Bella was choking him. The thought of Dimitry stabbing his daughter kept forcing it's way to the front of his mind. Powell wondered what Bella would be thinking if she could see him now, eating and drinking with Dimitry, as if they were friends. Powell had a compelling urge to put an end to the pretence and instead batter Dimitry into a pulp. He had to regularly remind himself to reign in those feelings. If he surrendered to the primeval urge for revenge it would be for his satisfaction, not the justice Bella would seek.

Bella had an almost naïve belief in the law and that justice would always prevail. If she was watching from above, she would be learning a great deal of new information about her father as Powell had never shared anything about his past in MI5, or the reasons for Vanessa's death. He had always dreaded her finding out about her mother's death as he was sure she would never forgive him.

Powell was doing everything possible to ensure Dimitry would come to England and so, despite hating his company, joined him for dinner.

"I was speaking with my associates and they are looking forward to seeing you, Dimitry," Powell said, after a couple of Tuicas to start the evening. "We are making a very special film next week and I think you would enjoy watching it being made."

"A film, Danny, sounds interesting. What sort of film exactly?"

"My associates make all types of films but this is special. We take an innocent young white girl and lock her in a room for a few hours with about six large black men, who proceed to enjoy her every way possible. The men are not gentle with the girl but I'm not saying any more because it will spoil the event."

"I like the sound of your film. Which day is it being filmed?"

"We were thinking of Tuesday or Wednesday. My associates also said they would like to talk business with you. They are always looking for more girls for their films and I told them I thought you might be able to help them?" Powell dangled the carrot and didn't have long to wait for a bite!

"Of course I can help them. I can find the right girls for everything."

"Exactly what I told them, Dimitry. This is additional business to what we have going on. I don't get involved in the film making side of the business." Powell could see Dimitry's eyes light up at the thought of further large deals for girls.

"I think I must come and meet your film friends," Dimitry said, pouring further glasses of Tuica. "To films," he toasted.

"To films," Powell raised his glass and downed the drink in one as was now the custom. "Will you be able to make it to England okay with the problems you mentioned?"

"They are nothing but a misunderstanding. I will come on Tuesday. I will fly to Gatwick and visit Brighton to see Stefan. But on Wednesday I will keep the day free to spend with you watching a film being made."

Powell felt a great sense of relief. In just three days he would be able to claim justice for Bella. "More Tuica," he urged. "And where are the girls? We should not drink alone. We have to celebrate."

CHAPTER TWENTY NINE

Afina awoke on Sunday morning with only a small hangover. Her mouth was dry but she had no headache. What she did have was a very bad feeling of guilt, having dreamed about Lia. Three men had been using Lia for sex and she had been looking at Afina accusingly, asking her to make them stop. The worst part about the dream for Afina was she was filming the sex and directing the men, telling them what to do to Lia. She didn't understand the dream as she wanted to help Lia not be part of her suffering.

A more immediate worry pushed thoughts of Lia to the back of her mind. Mara had discovered where she was staying. At least Afina had been careful not to mention her family were also staying above the bar. She wanted to speak to her friends and find out how the rest of the evening had gone, not whether they all had sex but did Mara say anything of importance. It was too early to call but she sent a text to each of them asking them to call when they were up and about. Then she organised breakfast for her mama and Adriana.

The apartment was full of memories of Bella. There were many pictures on the walls and furniture serving to remind Afina of how pretty she had been and so young to die. Afina wished Powell had removed the pictures but understood why he had not. He did not want to erase her memory but the pictures were a permanent reminder to Afina of the role she had played in Bella's death.

It had been difficult explaining to her mama about Bella's murder. When she convinced her mama to come to England, she had told her the full story. It had been necessary because her mama had not wanted to leave Bucharest. She had wanted to simply call the police and put a new, stronger lock on the front door. That was when Afina had realised she needed to tell her mama the truth, to convince her to come to England. They were all in danger from men who trafficked girls for sex, men who destroyed lives and killed without any remorse. Adriana was in terrible danger if they stayed. Once that realisation set in, her mama had immediately agreed to leave her home.

Afina had omitted the very worst parts about her rape and beating, saying she had escaped when she realised what was going to happen to her if she stayed. Then she had described how Bella sacrificed her life that Afina might run away and live. Her mama had wept on the phone and again when she arrived at the apartment and saw the pictures everywhere of Bella.

Afina's phone announced a message from Powell saying he would be back at the bar about lunchtime. She was happy with that news as she had been worried something might happen to him in her homeland and then she would have felt further guilt but even worse, at a complete loss what to do without him. Powell had been vague about why he was going to Bucharest but she assumed he was looking for Dimitry. She couldn't wait for his return to find out whether he had found Dimitry.

It was after eleven when Afina's phone rang and she recognised the number as belonging to Stefan. She stood staring at the number wondering how he had found her. What had Mara told him? Then she recovered her senses and remembered Stefan always had her number and didn't answer despite her curiosity as to why he was calling. A few seconds later she had a message telling her she had a voicemail. She nervously dialled her voicemail, almost afraid to hear Stefan's voice, as if somehow just listening to his message was dangerous.

The message was simple. "Afina, this is Stefan. Please call me urgently. If you don't call you won't like what happens to your family."

Afina smiled as she deleted the message. So Stefan doesn't yet know that my family are in England and out of his reach. That is good. That is very good. Thirty minutes later her phone rang again and this time it was Mara calling.

"I bet you've called me to tell me how you fucked my friends senseless," Afina answered.

There was a few seconds of silence at the other end and then she recognised Stefan's voice. "I wondered if you would answer if I used Mara's phone instead of mine to call you but what is this about her fucking your friends?"

Afina was lost for words. She was annoyed with herself for being trapped so easily by Stefan. "I meant Danny and my other customers," Afina answered. "I assume Mara is now getting to fuck them all?"

"Where are you Afina? You need to come back. And where is Victor?"

"Why do you ask me where is Victor? The last time I saw him he had my letter and I was running for my life, so why in hell's name would I know where he is? And as for coming back, you must be joking. You let Victor frighten me to death and then he promised to give me a hundred strokes of his cane when we reached the house. I ran for my life and I'm not coming back!"

She hoped she sounded convincing about Victor. It was at least the truth that she had no idea where he was. Powell had moved him somewhere and she couldn't even be sure he was still alive. She didn't believe Powell would just have killed Victor in cold blood but she wasn't going to lose any sleep worrying about whether he had or not.

"So where is he then?" Stefan asked.

"I hope the pig is dead," Afina responded angrily. "And you're no better. You promised to protect me from him but you were willing to see him beat me to death."

"Look Afina, come back to work and I promise there will be no beatings. Danny is now my business partner and he really likes you. We can make good money together."

"And what about my family? Was it Dimitry who threatened to rape Adriana?"

"Dimitry will hurt your family if you don't come back," Stefan warned. "You don't want him fucking your little sister."

"And if I do come back you will hurt me. Anyway, my family has moved. You won't find them."

"Afina, you are making more trouble for yourself. You were making good money with me…"

"And so were you," Afina interrupted sharply. "I am not coming back. Just forget about me." She pressed the end call button.

CHAPTER THIRTY

Stefan turned to Mara and handed back her phone.

"Afina says she is not coming back. I need to find her and I need to find Victor. Dimitry will be here in a couple of days and you know how close he is to Victor."

"What did Afina say happened to Victor?"

"She says she ran away from him and doesn't know where he is but I don't believe her."

"Perhaps he has had an accident and is in hospital? Afina is good at running away so she is probably telling the truth."

"Maybe but I need to ask her in person before I know for certain."

"You mean you want to hurt her. Afina is a nice girl, just leave her alone. You have plenty more girls."

"Mara, where is she?"

"I told you, I don't know," Mara retorted angrily. "I went to the bar last night but she never appeared. She's probably in hiding if she's got any sense and I hope you never find her."

"The first part of my call with Afina was interesting. She thought I was you and said something about you calling to tell her how you fucked her friends. Which friends was she referring to?"

"I don't know. Perhaps she meant Danny?"

"That's what she said but she wouldn't call Danny a friend. He was a customer not a friend. I'm thinking you did see Afina in the bar and she was with some friends. I know you like girls so perhaps you went home with them? I don't know what happened but something in your version of events isn't right. So how about you tell me the truth, otherwise it will be Dimitry asking the questions."

"Don't talk to me like that. I'm not one of your stupid girls, I'm your cousin. Fuck you and fuck Dimitry." Mara turned and stormed out of Stefan's apartment.

Afina was relieved when Powell returned. She felt more secure when he was close to hand. She had been shocked when he took the gun from his safe and confidently dealt with Victor but when he explained he used to work for the government she was very happy. This was a man who was not afraid of Victor or Dimitry or anyone else she suspected.

She immediately told Powell about her call from Stefan and the fact Mara knew where she was staying. He was concerned about Mara because even if she would not volunteer information to Stefan, it would be a completely different matter if Dimitry started applying painful pressure.

"You like Mara?" Powell asked.

"Yes and although I am not one hundred per cent sure I can trust her, I am worried I have caused her trouble with Stefan. It was stupid of me how I answered my phone."

"Dimitry is coming to England the day after tomorrow and will be in Brighton. He is going to be looking for Victor. If he suspects Mara knows something, I am sure he will get it out of her."

"But she is Stefan's cousin."

"I don't think that will matter. Look are you sure Mara doesn't know your family are here or that I own this place."

"I am sure."

"So the most she can do is point him here because she thinks you work here."

"Can't the police arrest him as soon as he arrives?"

"Possibly but I don't know for sure how he plans to get here. I offered to collect him from the airport but he said it wasn't necessary. Maybe he's not flying. I've arranged to spend Wednesday with him so that was when I was going to arrange for him to be arrested."

"What should we do?"

"For a start I think you need to stay out of sight until Wednesday. I'm going to talk to a friend about the welcoming arrangements for Dimitry."

"Once Dimitry is arrested, can we try and find Lia?"

"Once Dimitry is in custody the police will close down Stefan's business and try to track the girls like Lia."

"What are the chances of finding her?"

"Average at best but don't give up, I'll see what I can do as well."

"Thanks, Powell, I don't know what I would do without you."

Dinner had been excellent. They had all chosen from the menu and the food had been delivered upstairs to the apartment. Powell had announced he was going to be sleeping in the bar for the next forty eight hours as he didn't want to leave Afina and her family by themselves. Mama and Adriana went to bed early leaving Afina and Powell sitting next to each other on the sofa in the living room. They were sharing a bottle of wine and Afina had been telling Powell about her childhood.

Emboldened by the wine, Afina decided to ask something that she had been wondering about for some time, "What happened to Bella's mother?"

Powell didn't rush to answer. Afina could see the sadness in his eyes as he remembered the past and begun to wish she hadn't asked.

"She was killed by terrorists when Bella was just a baby," Powell finally answered.

"I'm so sorry, I had no idea."

"Life has a way of dealing us unexpected blows. You know that yourself."

"I guess I do. One month ago I was living a very quiet, normal life in Bucharest."

Afina was thoughtful for a minute as she sipped her wine. She turned to Powell and kissed him on the lips, gently and then probing with her tongue. He responded but not overly passionately.

"Don't you want to kiss me?" she asked after a minute. "Is it because of what I did, selling my body?"

"Of course not. I find you incredibly attractive but you're very vulnerable... and young."

"This isn't me working. I want you and I don't give a damn about the age difference." She leaned in and kissed him again. This time he responded more passionately. "That's better," she smiled.

"I'm afraid you're doing this for the wrong reasons. You don't owe me anything."

"Actually, I owe you everything but that isn't why I want to sleep with you. I like you and I like your body."

"I'll tell you what," Powell said. "If you still want me after we've dealt with Dimitry, then you won't have to ask twice." He kissed her passionately on the lips for a final time. "I'm going to bed," he announced.

As Powell walked off to sleep alone he was impressed with his restraint.

He really did find Afina very attractive and he felt a definite connection but he was worried it was brought on by his loss of Bella. He was sure they both needed some time to pass so they could see if their feelings were real or just the result of recent events.

In his office, which was also going to be where he slept for the next couple of nights, he decided it was time to call Brian Cooper. He didn't yet exactly need the cavalry but he did need some help. He couldn't be in a dozen places all at once.

CHAPTER THIRTY ONE

Mara thought about it all morning and finally decided to send Afina a text message warning her Dimitry would be returning to Brighton the next day. Then she hurriedly deleted all trace of the text. Stefan had avoided her since their argument the previous afternoon but she knew she needed to be cautious.

She had enjoyed having sex with Becky and Emma but it was Afina she had really wanted to spend the night with. There was just something indefinable about Afina that she couldn't resist. Now Mara was wishing she didn't know where Afina was staying. She wouldn't ever tell Stefan but he wouldn't dare hurt her. Dimitry was a completely different proposition, especially as he was desperate to find Victor.

Mara wondered if she should do the same as Afina and simply run away but that wasn't really practical as she couldn't avoid Stefan and her family forever. It would also make her appear guilty and so she decided she would keep to her story, deny any knowledge of where Afina was living and wait for things to go back to normal. Hopefully Stefan would stop Dimitry getting out of order if the need arose.

Mara had to spend the evening working as there were already three bookings and there would also be a number of others who would call at the last minute so for a Monday it looked like being busy. She was getting fed up of sucking and fucking random strangers. She'd done two years and had enough money put away to soon go back home and buy her own apartment. If she gave up working maybe she would have a chance with Afina, though she was going to take some convincing. Mara thought Afina had some bisexual tendencies but she certainly wasn't a full blown lesbian.

The doorbell rang announcing her first appointment and she went to answer. She was surprised and pleased when she found Danny standing on the doorstep.

"Hello Danny, Stefan didn't tell me it was you coming."

"It's good to see you again, Mara."

She led the way to her bedroom. "So how long do you want to stay? I'm afraid Afina isn't here so we can't have a threesum. Then again you probably know Afina isn't here and that's the only reason you're seeing me," she said teasing.

"Actually I came just to see you, Mara." He passed over one hundred pounds.

Mara counted the money and smiled. "An hour, sure you are up to it?"

She left the room for a minute but was quickly back again. She was obviously surprised he had made no attempt to start getting undressed. "Still fully clothed?"

"There's no hurry. Stefan tells me you are his cousin."

"And he tells me you are his new business partner."

"That's true. So tell me, where's Afina?"

"No idea so tell Stefan the answer is the same whether he asks or you ask for him!"

"Actually, I'm asking purely for myself. I'm glad to hear you haven't told Stefan where she is because I get the impression she's in trouble and I don't want her to come to any harm as I really like her."

"Sorry, I thought Stefan was using you to find out where she is, not that I know where she is anyway."

Powell decided to risk everything, "I know you know where to find Afina. What worries me is that you might be persuaded to tell Stefan or Dimitry."

"And why do you think I know where to find Afina?"

"Because the night before last you were with Afina, Becky and Emma drinking in a bar in Hove."

Mara looked shocked, "How do you know that?"

"Because she told me. Just like she told me Stefan called her yesterday on your phone."

"I don't understand. Why haven't you told Stefan?"

"I wish to protect Afina. She also wants me to protect you. She felt she put you in danger the way she answered your phone call yesterday."

"She didn't know it was Stefan calling."

"She is still feeling bad. She is desperate to ensure you come to no harm."

Mara couldn't help but smile. It was good to hear that Afina was so concerned for her safety but she was confused by Danny. "Why is Afina so important to you?" she asked.

"My reasons for protecting Afina are personal." He didn't plan to share more than he had to with Mara.

"Is she going to be working for you?"

"Not in the sense you mean. Anyway, I actually did have a purpose for coming here and it isn't to have sex with you."

"So why did you come?"

Powell took two miniature but powerful transmitters from inside his coat pocket. Each looked like and was the size of a cigarette lighter with a range of about three hundred metres. They had been a gift from Brian Cooper. "If we put one of these in your room and another in Stefan's living room, then I will be able to hear what is happening and help will come running if necessary."

Powell glanced around the room before placing the transmitter behind a picture on the mantelpiece. "I'm going to see Stefan shortly and I'll place this second one somewhere in his living room."

"Who are you, Danny?"

"A friend, Mara."

"You are not really going into business with Stefan, are you?"

"My organisation is happy to work with Stefan but I have a particular interest in Dimitry. It is a personal matter."

"Like with Afina?"

"Yes, like with Afina."

"Stefan is my cousin. He can be a shit sometimes but I wouldn't want him to get hurt."

Powell knew he had to tread carefully. "Stefan is my new business partner," he assured Mara. "With Victor and Dimitry out of the way, I believe Stefan and I can have a more fruitful partnership in the future."

"So you have killed Victor," Mara exclaimed. "And you plan to kill Dimitry?"

"I've told you too much already. I will help you if you promise not to tell Dimitry how to find Afina."

"I have no love for Victor or Dimitry. They can both rot in hell but Afina is a different matter. I really like Afina."

"And she likes you. So I will go see Stefan now and tell him we had great sex. Once Dimitry is out of the way, Afina will be able to see you again."

CHAPTER THIRTY TWO

Powell had rented a small but clean hotel room on Regency Square, just a short walk from Stefan's building and well within the range of the transmitter. He had moved Afina and her family out of the bar and into his house. After seeing Mara, he had been able to plant the second transmitter in Stefan's living room and in the first few hours he had heard nothing of great interest, though there had been the sounds of Mara having sex with various men, which had made him smile at first and then feel decidedly uncomfortable.

It did occur to Powell that if men didn't pay for sex then girls like Afina wouldn't end up being trafficked. It was all a case of supply and demand but realistically there would always be the demand. What he didn't understand was why the police weren't doing more to stop the trade. He had quite quickly found and infiltrated Stefan's business. No doubt the police would claim they were undermanned and underfunded but surely the misery caused by trafficking girls should place the crime very high on the list for focus and resources.

Sitting alone with time to spare was something Powell normally tried to avoid. His thoughts would inevitably turn to what might have been. He was continually haunted by the events of the past but now there was a more recent past trying to invade his mind with doubts and blame. He wasn't a religious man but often prayed for forgiveness. Exactly who he was praying to he wasn't sure.

It was now almost midnight and Dimitry was due to arrive the next day. Powell needed to sleep to be sharp for the next couple of days. Normally, he worked out at least every other day but had attended only two kickboxing classes in ten days. He had heard Stefan leave the room at about eight and return about eleven, after which everything went quiet in his room and Powell assumed he had gone to bed. Powell set his alarm for six and turned down the receiver so he could sleep without listening to any more grunts and groans coming from Mara's room.

When Powell awoke, he turned up the receiver but there was only silence at the other end, so he grabbed a quick shower and turned on the kettle provided to make some tea. He was reminded of many hours in the past spent on stakeouts but in those days he nearly always had a partner for company, which made getting something to eat a great deal easier.

As the hours dragged by, Powell realised neither Stefan or Mara were early risers. It was eleven when reception phoned to let him know Brian Cooper was on the way up to his room.

"Just like the old days," Brian said, as he entered the room laden with sandwiches and coffees. "This is Marius," he said, indicating the man who had followed him into the room.

"Good to see you, Brian, I'm starving."

Powell shook Marius's hand. "Nice to meet you Marius. I assume you're our translator?"

Marius was skinny and young, probably in his late twenties and wearing an ill-fitting brown suit. "Pleased to meet you," he replied. He spoke good English with only a little accent.

"I'm not sure exactly how much we might need you so I hope you've brought something to read."

"I have my kindle, thank you."

Brian put the food and coffees down on the table. "So what's happening?" he asked.

"Nothing much. Stefan is up and about but Mara hasn't stirred."

"And it was Mara you were telling me is in danger because she knows Afina is at your bar?"

Powell was quickly devouring the ham and cheese sandwich, and just nodded with a full mouth. He removed the plastic lid from the coffee and washed down the food. "I've moved Afina and her family to my place so they should be safe for the time being."

"Afina's family?"

"It's a long story but I had to get Afina's mother and sister out of Romania, as their lives were in danger and there really wasn't anywhere else for them to go."

"Well you've certainly been busy. I am a bit worried we have Dimitry in the house and don't arrest him immediately. A feeling shared by the local police."

"He is going to be just with me tomorrow and it will be easier to arrest him. If the police go in mob handed today, he won't surrender and more officers could be killed. I don't want that to happen and I don't want Mara or Stefan hurt either. We need to find out from Stefan where the other girls have been trafficked and who else is involved. That won't happen if he gets killed in a shootout.

Powell noticed Marius had stopped reading and was giving them his full attention. What he was hearing had probably come as something of a shock.

"I understand where you're coming from but we need to get this right," Brian warned. "Still, I haven't had as much fun in years, beats the hell out of training!"

Powell had been surprised his friend ended up behind a desk and wondered just how much he was to blame for that or perhaps he should be saying how much credit should he take. He may have saved his friend's life by his own misfortunes at least partly leading to Brian deciding to take a safe job.

The receiver made them both fall silent and listen as they clearly heard a male voice enter a room and say, 'Hello' before being met with a response in Romanian neither of them understood.

"That's Dimitry just arrived," Powell confirmed. "And Stefan is the other voice. What are they saying Marius?"

"The second man asked if Dimitry had a good flight."

Dimitry continued speaking Romanian. Powell heard Afina's name mentioned. "What is he saying about Afina?"

Marius translated, "He asked if there was any progress with finding the bitch, Afina."

There was some further conversation in Romanian and both Powell and Brian waited expectantly for a translation.

'Stefan says, he thinks someone called Mara knows where Afina is staying. He has told Dimitry to get a bit rough with this Mara and she'll tell him where to find Afina. Or if not Afina at least she knows where to find some of her friends.'

Powell wondered how Mara would react if she knew Stefan was throwing her to the proverbial wolf that was Dimitry.

Marius continued translating. "Dimitry says he thinks it's best he talks to Mara by himself."

Powell gave Brian a worried look. "This could turn nasty for Mara."

Marius continued, "Now Stefan has agreed but he has told Dimitry to be careful because he doesn't want to have to explain to his uncle how she died." Marius shot Powell a concerned look. "What are we going to do about this?"

"Just translate," Powell replied. "You're doing a good job."

They could hear a door close and a minute later they heard a knock on the door as the transmitter in Mara's room picked up Dimitry's arrival outside.

Powell and Brian both crouched forward as they heard the door open and listened to Mara greeting Dimitry as if he'd never been away. Powell was impressed with her coolness considering she knew he was there to potentially do her harm.

'Dimitry is telling her, Stefan has said she knows where to find Afina but won't say."

Powell could tell from Dimitry's tone of voice he was threatening Mara.

"Mara says she doesn't know where to find Afina. She does know one bar she has been to before when Stefan had her follow Afina but when she returned last time there was no sign of Afina."

Brian turned to Powell in shock when they both heard the crack of what must have been Dimitry's hand on Mara's face and the noise of her falling to the floor.

Marius was translating as fast as he could and looking nervously at Powell. 'Dimitry is threatening to break every bone in her body if she doesn't tell him how to find Afina." Marius threw his hand to his mouth in shock. "He has said, Stefan says he can't kill her but before he is finished with her, she will be begging him to kill her.'

"This is going to be worse than I thought," Powell said turning to Brian.

"Shall I call the cavalry?"

"No," Powell responded firmly. "At least not yet."

"We must call the police," Marius urged, then returned to translating. "Mara says she can't tell him what she doesn't know. She is very brave, she just swore at him."

Powell might not understand Romanian but as Mara increased her shouting at Dimitry, he knew she was calling him every name under the sun. There was a sudden further scream of pain.

Marius continued, 'Dimitry is again threatening her, she will tell him how to find Afina eventually so she might as well save herself the pain. Mara is begging him not to hurt her."

"Help me. Please someone help me!" Mara screamed out in English.

Powell decided he must intervene. Mara knew he was listening and she was pleading for his direct help.

"I can't listen to any more of this," Powell' announced. "I'm going round there."

Powell ran from the hotel room and down the four flights of stairs before Brian could answer. In just two minutes he was standing in front of the familiar door ringing the bell. At the same time he dialled Stefan. "I'm downstairs, answer the bloody door," he demanded when Stefan answered. "It's important."

Stefan was at the door just a few seconds later.

"Hi Danny, I wasn't expecting to see you today. What's so important?"

Danny followed Stefan into the house and closed the door. "I think I've seen Afina," Powell said, as he followed Stefan up the stairs and came close to the door to Mara's room.

Stefan stopped and made the decision to immediately knock on Mara's door. "It's me," he said loudly.

Dimitry opened the door and Powell could see behind him Mara was lying on the bed semi-naked and looking distraught. There was blood running from a split lip.

"Danny, it's good to see you again," Dimitry said. "Mara here is being very obstinate. She won't tell us how to find Afina."

"Danny says he's seen her," Stefan announced.

"Really," Dimitry smiled. "Where was this?"

"In Hove this morning. I was at the supermarket and I saw her getting in a car. I called out to her and she looked at me. It was definitely her but she got in the car and they drove away."

"Who was she with?"

"I'm not sure but to be honest he looked a bit like you guys. You know, he was tall, dark and swarthy looking, mid-thirties I'd guess and he had a scar on his neck."

"That's Victor," Dimitry exclaimed.

"What is she doing with him?" Stefan asked.

"I have no idea," Dimitry admitted. "What car was he driving?"

"It was a smart BMW," Powell answered.

"Victor doesn't own a car in England. Does he?" Stefan asked uncertainly.

"No," Dimitry answered. "This doesn't make sense."

"Perhaps he has fallen in love with Afina and they have run off together,"

Powell suggested. "Afina could definitely tempt me to do something stupid."

"Victor can have any woman he wants. Whatever is going on it has nothing to do with love, I am sure of that!"

"Then perhaps he is going into business with Afina," Powell suggested, intent on stirring the pot.

"I have no fucking idea what he is doing," Dimitry answered angrily. "But the answer is to find Afina. I need to encourage Mara a little further. You go upstairs and I will join you soon."

"Dimitry, I have some experience of finding things out from people who don't want to speak," Powell responded. "Perhaps I could have the pleasure of asking Mara what she knows? The films we make for our special guests often involve a severe interview of an unwilling girl. I'd actually quite enjoy breaking Mara. Why don't you guys go upstairs and leave me with her for say twenty minutes. That should be long enough."

"Please don't leave me with Danny," Mara shrieked. "He's told me about how he likes to hurt women."

Perfectly on cue, Powell thought. Mara would make a damn good actress.

"Well it seems Mara is more afraid of you than me," Dimitry acknowledged. "I need to take a piss and get a coffee. You can have her for twenty minutes and if you have no luck we will try again together."

Powell breathed a sigh of relief. "It will be my pleasure to extract what you need to know," he promised. "I am hoping she is stronger than she looks, otherwise it will be no fun."

"Don't kill her," Stefan warned. "She's family."

"She will be returned to you alive if not very well," Powell confirmed.

Stefan and Dimitry headed up the stairs and Powell entered Mara's room.

"Are you okay?" Powell asked.

"Yes but I wouldn't have been if you hadn't arrived," Mara answered, sitting up on the bed. "What do we do now?"

"I'm going to tell them you met Afina at a lap dancing club where she was thinking of working. You chatted up a couple of other girls, who were both lesbian and you all had some drinks and dances from the girls. You left with the other girls because Afina wasn't interested in joining you for sex. You were pretty drunk and can't even remember their names let alone where they lived. Afina said she was going to speak to the manager about getting a job as a dancer. The name of the club is Bunnies. Do you remember all that?"

"Yes but will Dimitry believe me?"

"I'm just trying to buy us some time."

"I hope it works. I'm not brave. If Dimitry really hurts me I will tell him everything I know. I won't want to but I won't be able to help myself."

"I understand but we are listening in so if anything gets out of hand we can be here in less than five minutes."

"You are a good actor Danny."

"What do you mean?"

"The first time I met you I thought you were a shy nobody. That isn't you at all."

"If I remember rightly, you were the better actor that first time, pretending you enjoyed yourself with me."

"You were a good customer, polite and easy so it was for me a good time."

"Okay so now I need some more acting from you. In the minute I'm going to need some realistic screaming."

"What are you going to do?" Mara asked slightly apprehensively.

"Something extremely painful that leaves no visible marks."

Mara's first attempt at screaming was a little underwhelming but she warmed to the task and if anyone was listening they would have been convinced she was suffering horribly.

Powell joined the others upstairs about twenty minutes later and recounted the story he had agreed with Mara.

"How did you get her to tell you that so quickly?" Dimitry asked.

"Easy really. I guess you hit her a couple of times and then asked questions. I introduced her to a more prolonged form of pain although some people find it pleasurable. I held her down and started fisting her, which she accommodated with some screaming. I then started on her arse and she quickly gave up the information."

"Is she okay?" Stefan asked.

"A bit sore probably but otherwise okay. I didn't make much progress with her arse before she was begging me to stop."

"I like your style, Danny," Dimitry said admiringly. "Do you know this Bunnies club where Mara saw Afina?"

"I've heard of it but I've not been there."

"I will pay it a visit tonight," Dimitry stated. "See if Afina is working and speak to the manager."

"I'll come with you," Danny suggested. "But we mustn't have too late a night. I have a big day planned for tomorrow."

CHAPTER THIRTY THREE

Powell started the day by meeting with Brian and Chief Inspector Brown at Brighton police station. There was a sense of nervous excitement in the room as the Chief Inspector learned he was about to arrest Bella's killer and solve a crime that had become increasingly likely to end up adding to the unsolved crime statistics. Brown was far from happy at first to learn Powell had been chasing around Europe, trying to locate Dimitry on his own but was pragmatic enough to reign in his feelings, once he realised he was being handed Dimitry on a proverbial platter. The icing on the cake was Afina's willingness to testify to what she had seen. The Chief Inspector could see he would have a cast iron case.

Brian had shown his credentials and explained he was a friend of Powell and had been Bella's Godfather but stressed he was not present in any official capacity.

"I'm acting more as a character witness, so you take Powell seriously," Brian explained.

"So where are you meeting Dimitry?" the Chief Inspector asked.

"One thing first, I need you to arrest Dimitry but help me make it appear I have managed to escape," Powell explained.

"And why might that be?" the Chief Inspector enquired with a quizzical look.

"There are some associates of Dimitry who are involved in a number of illegal activities and I want to be free to pursue them further."

The Chief Inspector was thoughtful for a moment. "I guess we could arrange that. I can't say I approve of what you're doing but it certainly appears to have been effective so far."

"Powell is always very effective," Brian added.

Powell smiled, "I try to be," he said.

"And how exactly did you come to know Powell, Mr Cooper?"

"A long time ago we were in a similar line of work. Suffice it to say, if I was ever in a sticky situation, he would be the first person I would want at my side."

"I see where Bella got her guts from," the Chief Inspector commented. "So is there anything else I should know?"

Powell responded, "When you interview Afina you are going to find she was trafficked into the country and put to work as a prostitute here in Brighton. There have been many other girls before her and I've told Afina I will try and trace what has happened to one girl in particular. Once you have Dimitry, I just need a little time to start looking. Along the way I expect to identify a network of Dimitry's associates all over the country who are forcing girls to work for them in brothels. You won't learn anything from Dimitry but think I can leverage his arrest to get even closer into his organisation."

"I need to pass this up the line but based on what you've achieved so far I don't see why there should be any opposition. I do need your assurance there is no question of a sudden outbreak of violence on the streets of Brighton," the Chief Inspector stressed. "After everything that's happened, I don't want to have to come arrest you one day. And Bella wouldn't want that either."

"I'm just doing some unofficial leg work. I can go places and do things the police can't but as you've seen with Dimitry, you guys get to make the arrest."

"Okay, so where do we make all this happen?"

"I'm picking him up at ten and driving up the A23 to London. I thought a service station may be suitable, perhaps the first one you hit near the Henfield exit?"

"It's a possibility but we need to prepare and keep the public at arm's length as much as we can." The Chief Inspector looked at his watch. "We have about two hours to get ready, should be enough time. Do you expect him to be armed?"

"I think that's doubtful but I can't be certain. Given his history, I think we should assume he will be carrying a knife."

"Indeed. So have you thought about how we are going to let you escape?" the Chief Inspector enquired.

"When I go to pay for the petrol you need to move in on Dimitry. I'll spot what is happening and just before I enter the shop I'll jump in the nearest car, which you will have left for me with the keys in the ignition. Dimitry should see me escape and believe I'm not involved."

"He might still be suspicious when he thinks about it later. He'll wonder why you chose to stop where you did and how we seemed ready for him."

"You need to make it look like you have been following him."

"We'll have two cars follow you into the service station and just use them to make the arrest. In case anything goes wrong we'll have other officers pretending to be the public and working in the shop but they won't show their hand unless it becomes absolutely necessary. I think that's the best we can do."

"I'll call you later to confirm details, Chief Inspector. With surprise on our side it should all go smoothly."

Powell collected Dimitry as arranged and they drove twenty minutes to the service station. The previous evening they had visited the Bunnies club but there had obviously been no sign of Afina and the manager admitted he auditioned so many girls he couldn't remember one from the other. They had stayed long enough to enjoy a few beers and a couple of dances from very average looking girls before Powell announced he was leaving and saving himself for the next day. Dimitry had also had enough and the agreement was reached to meet at ten outside Stefan's house.

Powell and Brian had taken shifts listening to the microphones to make sure Dimitry didn't decide to start asking further questions of Mara but the airwaves had remained quiet.

Powell drove at a steady pace and feigned surprise he needed to fill up with petrol shortly after joining the A23. Dimitry seemed disinterested in conversation and was slumped back in his chair half asleep.

Powell pulled into the service station and was pleased there were no signs of the ambush that was being prepared. He stepped out the car and glanced behind as a couple of other cars drove in and parked at the adjacent petrol pumps. He put thirty pounds of unleaded in his BMW and then started to walk towards the shop to pay.

Although he was expecting what happened next it still made him jump as he heard several police officers descend on his car, shouting at the occupant to get out and lie on the ground.

At least two of the policemen were pointing guns at Dimitry. At the sound of the first shout, Powell had run for the car at the front pump where a man was filling the car with petrol. Powell ignored the man's protestations, assuming he was in any case a policeman, and pushed him out of the way before jumping into the driver's seat. He accelerated away and in his rear view mirror could see the police already handcuffing Dimitry.

One car gave chase as he expected but after a few miles Powell slowed his speed and the car overtook. The driver gave him a wave as he went past and Powell left the A23 at the next exit. He drove a couple more miles then stopped at a bus stop. He took out his phone and called Stefan.

"Stefan, we have a big problem. The police have taken Dimitry prisoner. I was lucky to get away."

"What happened?"

"They must have followed us because when I stopped for petrol they drove in behind us and grabbed Dimitry, while I went to pay."

"How did you get away?"

Was that a hint of suspicion Powell detected in Stefan's voice? "I stole someone else's car and made a run for it. Only the one car chased me and I lost him. Luckily I know the roads real well. Last I saw they were putting handcuffs on Dimitry."

"The bloody fool shouldn't have come back. Where are you?"

"Somewhere near Hassocks. Do you think someone tipped off the police? How did they manage to find us?"

"Dimitry is the most wanted man in Brighton. Anyone could have spotted him and called the police. What are you going to do now?"

"I couldn't come and stay with you by any chance? Only they have my car and will have traced me as owner by now so I can't risk going home. I need to ditch this car damn quick and I could take a taxi back to your place."

There were a few seconds of quiet while Stefan considered the request. "Okay," he agreed. "Nothing connects me to either of you and Dimitry will never say anything."

"Thanks. I'll see you in about an hour."

Trafficking

CHAPTER THIRTY FOUR

Mara answered the door. "Hi Danny, Stefan's expecting you," she said smiling. "Just go straight up."

Powell hurried up the stairs and found Stefan in his lounge. He half expected Afina to appear from her bedroom.

"Thanks Stefan," Powell said by way of greeting.

"This is a complete fuck up," Stefan replied, rising from his chair. "First Victor and now Dimitry."

"My investors aren't best pleased. They are questioning whether I was right to invest in you guys, given what's now happened to Dimitry."

"I'm sorry, Danny. Dimitry was foolish coming back here so soon. Don't worry about your investors, I'm sure I can still supply the girls you want."

"That's good to hear because my investors aren't the sort of people I want to disappoint, if you know what I mean?"

"I understand exactly, Danny. I have similar men back home who do not tolerate failure. So we will not fail!"

"I think it would be helpful if I could understand more about how your business operates, Stefan. If Victor and Afina are plotting to take over your business then I think you may need my help as much as I need yours."

"Victor and Afina! You think they are responsible for the police arresting Dimitry?"

"It makes sense. With Dimitry out of the way, Victor and Afina can more easily go into competition with you."

Stefan was thoughtful for a few moments. "Victor and Dimitry are old friends, it doesn't make sense."

"Maybe Afina has turned Victor's head. He wouldn't be the first man to be so captivated by a woman he turns on his friends."

"True but I never understand why it happens. Another woman to fuck is easy to find but a good friend…"

"Let's have a coffee and you can tell me a bit more about your girls, then I can phone my investors and assure them everything is still under control and their money isn't at risk."

"I'll send Mara out for some. What do you like?"

"A large Latte please."

Twenty minutes later they were sat at the small table drinking their coffees and Powell was happy he was making progress. "I remember Afina mentioned she had a threesum with a girl called Lia, where did she end up?"

"She was just one of the girls I bring to Brighton and then sell on to someone else."

"My investors have operations all over the country. If our first collaboration goes well, I can see them wanting many more girls."

"That would be great, Danny. Finding the girls is never a problem. Finding a customer who can afford to pay our rates is more difficult."

"So as an example, where did Lia end up?"

"She went to a regular customer in Leeds. He has a couple of brothels and about a dozen girls."

"Do you deliver the girls or do they pick them up?"

"We deliver, it's part of the service. They only pay when we actually deliver the girls."

"Who do you use to deliver the girls?"

"Victor did most of the deliveries. I have a couple of girls here now and haven't found a replacement for Victor. I was hoping he would turn up sometime soon."

"Where do they need to go?"

"There is one for London and one for Leeds. Danny, you wouldn't be able to help would you?"

"Of course I can. I want to get out of Brighton for a bit anyway. How did Victor transport them?

"We give them something to make them easy to move and then you can just drive them."

"What do you give them?"

"We put some Rohypnol in a drink and they are like putty in your hands for twelve hours."

"Give me the details of where they need to go and I can take them this afternoon, if you want?" Powell thought it ironic he had used the same drug to make Victor easy to transport from his bar to the secure hospital unit.

"That would be brilliant Danny and I know Mike in Leeds will be happy to look after you for a couple of days. Maybe you would like to be the first to try the new girls?" Stefan slapped Powell on the back. "How about if I give you a couple of thousand for delivering each girl?"

"It's not really necessary, Stefan. We are partners and we help each other."

"I insist you take four thousand, partner or not. I am very happy to have met you, Danny. We will work well together."

CHAPTER THIRTY FIVE

Powell drove the two girls straight to his home where he had earlier warned Afina to expect the two arrivals. The girls needed helping from his car into the house as they were suffering the effects of the drugs they had been given by Stefan. Afina and her mother had prepared beds and it was only a few minutes before both girls were asleep.

When Powell agreed to deliver the girls, he had phoned Afina and told her to keep the girls safe for twelve hours, which was all the time he needed to drive to Leeds and locate Lia. He felt confident he would be able to pose as a customer and be with Lia at the same time Brian liaised with the police to organise a raid on the property. It was his intention that Brian should also feed the police details of the London brothel and Stefan's location, so a coordinated swoop could be made on all three addresses at the same time.

Confident the two girls were in good hands, Powell called Brian to give him the rough outline for his plan so he could prepare the police to take action. The police had at least six hours to prepare, which Powell reckoned should be enough time. Then he headed for the motorway and Leeds. He fed the post code given him by Stefan, into the Sat Nav system and settled back to listen to music.

The drive went quite well despite roadworks on the M1 and four hours later he was on the outskirts of Leeds. He didn't know the city but the post code had already informed him the house he wanted was in the Headingley suburb, which he did know was a famous cricket ground. He had spent some time on the internet before he left home, locating the brothel and the phone number. He had Mike's personal number from Stefan but had been right in his assumption it wasn't the advertised number for getting a girl.

He parked up on the side of the road and called the number. A man answered and Powell asked if he could arrange to see Lia for later that evening. He was prepared to say she had been recommended by a friend but the man at the end of the phone showed no surprise at his requesting Lia. He was booked in for ten, which would give the police a couple of hours to organise final details.

Powell called Brian and gave him the details, then he drove past the house, which turned out to be a very innocuous terraced house in a rather run down area. A few streets later Powell parked close to a pub advertising food as he hadn't eaten for hours.

Powell ordered his food and then called Afina to check on the girls. It had been approximately six hours since they were given the drugs and both of them were now awake but disorientated. Afina and her mother were comforting them and giving them coffee and some food. They were both over the moon at having been rescued.

Powell explained to Afina what he had arranged and told her to expect a call later to update her on events. Hopefully, Powell would be giving her the good news Lia was safe and Stefan in police custody. Then he called Brian to check everything was organised as expected. The raid on the three properties was confirmed for ten thirty.

CHAPTER THIRTY SIX

Powell arrived at the property and knocked at the door to be greeted by a middle aged woman.

"Come this way," she instructed with a smile, in a strong Yorkshire accent and led the way into a room off the hallway, which turned out to be a bedroom. "Have you been before?" she asked.

"No, it's my first time."

"I'll send the girls in and you can choose which you like."

"I specifically booked Lia," Powell said hurriedly, suddenly concerned he had made a long trip for nothing.

"Okay, I'll send Lia in once we've done the prices. It's fifty pounds for half an hour and one hundred pounds for an hour. You get a covered blow job and sex. Oral without is an extra twenty, as is kissing and anal is fifty. If you want something else then ask and I'll quote you a price. Everything is available." She reeled off the prices like an everyday shopping list.

"I'll have an hour please with oral without and kissing, so one hundred and forty?" He didn't plan to have anything so wasn't entirely sure why he didn't just take the minimum but he thought there might be some value in looking like a worthwhile customer. He started counting the money from his wallet and passed over the notes.

"Lia will be right in," the woman said after counting the money and hurried away.

Powell was left alone, wondering if he would recognise Lia from Afina's description. After about five minutes a girl walked in wearing just underwear. She smiled but not with her eyes. She seemed dazed and in something of a trance, which Powell attributed to her probably being on drugs.

"Thanks for asking for me," Lia said. "Have I seen you before?"

"No but you were highly recommended."

"I was?" Lia seemed surprised. "Who by?"

"Afina."

"Afina?" Lia looked confused. "Afina is a girl's name."

Powell was concerned she didn't immediately recognise Afina's name. Was this really Lia? "I'm a regular of Afina in Brighton. She said she once had a threesum with you and told me if I was ever up this way to ask for you."

The mention of Brighton had the desired effect.

"Afina. I know Afina. I liked her. She was kind to me."

Powell had to be certain. "What's the name of the man Afina works for? I don't like him."

"Stefan," Lia answered immediately. "I don't like him either." She undid her bra and looked inquisitively at Powell. "Aren't you going to get undressed?"

"I'm a bit odd," Powell explained. "I just like to look at you and talk a bit."

"But you paid for kissing and oral without?"

"I always pay for extras. I find it makes the girls friendlier."

"Well I'm feeling very friendly." She removed her knickers and started to rub her breasts provocatively. "Why don't you get comfortable on the bed and then you can talk as dirty as you like to me?"

Powell decided to do as suggested and lay on the bed with the pillow propped up behind his head. He couldn't help but notice that Lia had a very attractive body but he reminded himself to concentrate, within about twenty minutes he expected the police to arrive. "Take your time," he said, once he was comfortable. He felt it was safest to proceed as if he had weird sexual tastes rather than tell her the truth. She wasn't reliable in her drugged state.

Lia moved her hips suggestively and her hand moved from her now erect nipples to between her legs.

"That's nice," Powell encouraged but in truth his mind was miles away, thinking back on his life and wondering how the hell he came to be lying on this bed, instead of home with a family like most normal people.

"Don't you want to touch yourself?" Lia asked.

"I'm fine, thanks. I like looking at you." He checked his watch. Only ten minutes to go.

Lia started to simulate that she was actually enjoying playing with herself by breathing quicker and making pleasurable sounds.

In Powell's opinion, she would not make a great actress and he felt sorry for putting her through this charade. "Let's sit and talk a bit," he suggested.

Lia seemed relieved to be able to stop pretending she had an imminent climax approaching and slumped on the edge of the bed. "I'm sorry," she said. "You don't like me, do you?"

"I like you very much, Lia."

"Please tell the hostess you enjoyed being with me," she pleaded.

"Relax, in a few minutes this hell for you will be over and you won't have to worry anymore about pleasing hostesses or strange men."

Lia seemed not to have heard what he said. "Only if you don't say I was good he will beat me."

"Lia, listen to me." Powell moved from his prone position to sit next to her. He put his arm around her shoulder. "Put your clothes back on because we are going to be leaving here very soon."

"Have you bought me?" Lia asked.

"No Lia, I haven't bought you. I'm a friend. Afina sent me to get you out of here. I helped her escape from Stefan and she remembered she had promised to help you so she sent me up here to help you escape."

For the first time Powell saw the hint of something different in Lia's eyes, it was hope.

"You're going to get me out of here?" she asked. "Really?"

"In five minutes the police will be knocking on the door and you will be free. They will need to take a statement from you about everything that has happened to you and then you will be able to go home."

"To Romania?" Lia asked. Her eyes were positively ablaze now with hope and excitement.

"Yes to Romania."

Powell heard the front door being broken down and the footsteps of multiple people rushing into the house. "It's the police," he explained to a frightened Lia. "Quickly, put your underwear on."

The door to the room was opened and two police officers stood in the doorway surveying the inside.

"I'm Powell and this is Lia. Please get a female officer in here and find her some clothes."

He turned to Lia and could see a huge smile on her face. He took his phone from his pocket and called Afina.

After Powell had given Afina the good news about Lia and heard the two girls at home had gone back to bed but were both in good spirits, he then called Brian and learned Stefan had been taken into custody. The London raid had also gone well. The only person to evade the police was Mike, who hadn't been at the Leeds address when the place was raided.

It was a good result and Brian passed on the thanks of the very grateful police. Dimitry's arrest was the star event of the night's work but putting an end to trafficking actually was high on the police agenda so there were currently many happy senior police officers around the country, who owed Powell a debt of gratitude.

Powell had booked two rooms at the Hilton in the city centre and at one thirty in the morning he drove Lia back to the hotel. She had provided a statement to the police and was going to return next morning to help further with their questions.

The hotel rooms were adjacent on the third floor. As they stood outside the rooms he handed Lia her key. "Have a good night. I've ordered us alarm calls for nine and then we can go down to breakfast before visiting the police station again." He'd already told her that he would drive her down to Brighton to meet with Afina before flying back to Romania.

"I can't thank you enough," Lia said.

"Thank Afina, not me. It was her who made this happen."

Lia hesitated in front of her door. She started to insert the key card then stopped. "Can I stay with you tonight," she asked. "I don't want to be alone and I feel safe with you."

Powell was taken aback by the request. He thought she would be happy to finally have some time to herself but he could also understand she still felt scared and the weed she had been smoking each night would heighten her fears, although would be out of her system by the morning and she would be able to start rebuilding her life.

"Okay," Powell agreed. "I have two large beds anyway so I guess we can have one each."

"Thank you," Lia said, throwing her arms around him.

Powell went to bed feeling it had been a good day's work. He was pretty confident Bella would be proud of her father.

CHAPTER THIRTY SEVEN

On the advice of her solicitor, Mara had said little throughout the interview. She admitted she was Stefan's cousin but knew very little of his business dealings. She simply worked as an escort to earn a good living. If Stefan was trafficking girls, she knew nothing about it as he kept his business to himself. She had little sympathy for Stefan and none for Dimitry but she wouldn't testify against either of them, as her family back home would never sanction such an act of perceived treachery, which would inevitably lead to retribution. She knew her Uncle was not the type of man you disappoint, the stories about his brutality were legendary.

The police had offered immunity from prosecution if she would be a witness but she made it clear she would not be willing in any circumstances to testify. They could lock her up if necessary but she had joked there was more chance of England winning the world cup than her giving evidence. The policeman had understood that meant zero chance.

The police then tried threatening her with being arrested as an accomplice to trafficking but she reckoned it was just hot air to try and convince her to give them the statement they so desperately wanted, so she sat still and pleaded ignorance. She did ask the policeman if he wanted a list of her customers. She wouldn't be able to remember them all but she did know the names of a few senior police officers and a number of members of the judiciary, including at least two barristers and a judge. The policeman conducting the interview pointed out it was not her customers who were being charged with any crime but he had heard enough.

Twenty four hours after being taken to Brighton police station Mara was allowed to leave but informed she should expect to be called in for further questioning so she mustn't leave the area without first checking with the police whether it was okay. As she stood outside, she was uncertain at first what to do and where to go but realised the only person she really knew in Brighton, who wasn't currently in jail was Afina. She didn't want to go back to the empty building she had called home for the last two years so took out her phone and called Afina, suggesting they meet up at the bar but not for a couple of hours, as she needed to make some calls back home to explain what had happened.

Powell was half way down the motorway and Lia was asleep in the passenger seat when Brian rang.

"We have a potential problem," Brian said.

Powell became alert. He had been worrying everything was going too well. Most operations he remembered never went so smoothly. "What's wrong?"

"Unfortunately and rather unbelievably Victor is going to be released first thing tomorrow and there is nothing I can do about it."

While it was bad news, it had always been inevitable Victor would eventually be released, Powell just hadn't anticipated it being quite so quickly. "How come?"

"They have a new head of Psychiatry and he isn't someone we've dealt with before. It seems he's made a quick assessment that Victor is perfectly safe to be let out and return to Romania. Apart from anything else it seems beds are in short supply and the idea of shipping any further treatment costs for Victor to Romania, is a very attractive option and helps with their budgeting."

"Can we ensure he gets straight on a plane to Romania?"

"Not really, it isn't a mandated condition of his release so essentially he is free to come and go as he pleases."

"Couldn't he be charged with at the very least being an accessory to Stefan's trafficking business?"

"The police are trying to put a case together but at the moment there isn't any real evidence, as nobody is talking. Some of the girls have mentioned him driving them to their place of work but we can't arrest him for being a taxi driver."

Powell thought about asking Afina to make a statement accusing Victor of assault and rape but the charge would never stick, not without forensic evidence or witnesses. It would be her word against his and the prosecution would no doubt give her a torrid time in the witness box. It would be unfair, given what she had already gone through, to ask her to get involved with a case that had so little chance of being proven.

"What about the Romanian angle? Surely he's wanted over there for some crime?" Powell asked, hopefully.

"Seems not. He is known to the police out there but there's no current, outstanding warrants."

Powell was concerned Victor would come looking for him and Afina. He had hoped to have solved the problem of Afina's future before Victor's release so he would be the only one in any danger. Currently he had a house full of very vulnerable females and Victor could come visiting before lunch the next day. "I could do with some extra security at my house. Do you think the local coppers would be willing to post someone outside?"

"I've already spoken with them and they are so thankful for you handing them Dimitry, there will be two officers outside from tomorrow morning."

"Thanks, Brian. I'll try and get the girls out of danger and back home as soon as possible."

"That would be for the best. You've changed you know? The Powell of twenty years ago would have made Victor disappear permanently."

"You're not seriously saying I should have murdered Victor?"

"Not at all! I think you've changed for the better. Bella would be very proud of you."

"Thanks. I was very proud of her and though she didn't know it, she completely changed my life. In difficult situations I actually find myself thinking, what would Bella want me to do."

"I've also arranged for two other officers to track Victor to see if he does get on a plane," Brian added.

"When he finds out Dimitry and Stefan are locked up he will probably be on the first plane out of the country, at least he will if he's got any sense but you can't be too careful."

"My sentiments entirely," Brian agreed.

CHAPTER THIRTY EIGHT

Powell had returned with Lia just a short time before Afina was due to leave for the bar to meet Mara. There were hugs and tears as Lia thanked Afina for being a friend and not ignoring her plight. The two other girls, who had revealed their names to be Cosmina and Violette, were also thanking Powell for their rescue and at Afina's suggestion it was agreed they would all go to the bar to meet Mara and celebrate. Including Afina's mother and sister there were seven of them in total split between two taxis.

As soon as Powell arrived at the bar with six females in tow, the staff moved quickly to create a large enough table to seat them and Mara when she arrived. Powell ordered champagne and announced the party should commence. In truth, he was a little concerned about Victor being free next morning but he didn't want to worry any of the others and reckoned this might be the only chance for all of them to celebrate together before most of them returned to Romania.

Afina had a quiet word with Powell and he readily agreed to her suggestion that she invite Emma and Rebecca to join the celebration so by the time Mara arrived twenty minutes late, she was surprised to find a party in progress.

Introductions were made and Afina noticed broad smiles on the faces of Emma and Rebecca as they said hello to Mara. Afina was a little jealous of what they had shared together but despite liking all three girls and now considering them good friends, she simply preferred to have her sex with men.

She turned towards Powell and their eyes met for a second. She broke into a smile and then looked away afraid he might be able to read her thoughts, which at that moment were making her blush.

Powell was suddenly by her side. "A penny for them," he said.

"I don't understand?"

"In England we say, a penny for your thoughts. It means what are you thinking?"

"But why is it a penny?"

Powell was stumped for an answer. "I've no idea."

"My thoughts are worth much more than a penny."

"I'm sure they are."

"English is a strange language."

There was a silence between them for a few seconds as they both sipped their drinks.

"Have you thought about when you wish to fly home?" Powell asked. He didn't really want Afina to go home and knew if she did go, it was going to leave a vacuum in his life not easily filled by anyone else but he had to do what was best for Afina.

"Mama wants to go as soon as possible."

"And you?"

"I was thinking of staying. There is nothing for me in Romania. If you still have a job for me I would like to stay and get to know England properly."

"Of course you can have a job and you can stay in the flat if you want."

"That would be brilliant but I want to pay you rent for your flat. You have done enough for me already."

"Okay, we can discuss the amount later. Tomorrow we should talk to your mother and sister about going home."

"I'll talk to them, I need to tell them I'm planning to stay. I'm not sure my mother will be happy about the idea."

As a parent, Powell understood how Afina's mother might feel about the idea of again being separated from her daughter.

Mara walked towards them with a big grin on her face.

"Let me guess," Afina said. "You are going home with Emma and Rebecca."

"Unless you want me to stay with you two?" Mara asked with a naughty grin.

Powell answered first. "Mara, you are a bad influence!"

"Is that a no?"

"Yes it is a no," Powell confirmed, smiling.

"It seems strange calling you Powell," Mara said. "I liked Danny."

"Sorry I couldn't tell you before tonight."

"Don't apologise. Afina has told me the whole story. Bella was a very lucky girl to have you as her father. I would be very proud to call you my friend, if you can forgive me for my part in everything?"

"There's nothing to forgive. I already think of you as my friend."

"Thank you, Powell. That name is definitely going to take some getting used to."

Mara kissed both Powell and Afina on the cheeks.

Afina looked towards Emma and Rebecca and gave a small wave goodbye.

"I like Mara," Powell said after she had left.

"Of course you do. She is beautiful and sexy and…" Afina teased. "Would you like another threesum with us both?"

"Afina, this is Powell you're talking to not Danny."

"Can I ask you a question, Powell?"

"Of course."

"Why did you never remarry?"

"No one would have me," Powell answered flippantly.

"I don't believe that. I think many girls would love to be with you."

"I guess the truth is I didn't want to put anyone in harm's way. After what happened to Vanessa, I couldn't risk a repeat."

CHAPTER THIRTY NINE

Mara had only finally fallen asleep with the girls at about four in the morning. At nine thirty when her mobile rang, she couldn't be bothered to answer at first but someone refused to be ignored and after the third call she knew she had to untangle the legs wrapped around her and put an end to the ringing. She moved slowly out of bed, as the sex had been mixed with a large amount of alcohol and she was feeling the effects. She found her phone on the floor beside her clothes just as the caller rang for the fourth time.

She was shocked to see Victor's name as the caller and decided to ignore him, hoping he would go away. The phone rang again and she heard Emma telling her to answer the bloody thing.

"Hello Victor. Where have you been? Everyone has been looking for you."

"Where's Stefan? I need to speak with him urgently. Neither him or Dimitry are answering their phones."

"The police have arrested them both."

"What! How is that possible? Tell me what happened?"

Mara walked into the next room and sat on the sofa. She explained to Victor about Dimitry's capture and the police raid to take Stefan. She said nothing about Powell.

"I bet it was that bastard Powell," Victor swore.

"Why do you say that?"

There was a brief silence at the end of the phone before Victor replied. "It was him put me in a bloody hospital. Him and that Afina bitch."

"We never saw Afina again after she left with you."

"I'm not surprised. Are you at the house?"

"I've nowhere else to go," Mara said resignedly. "Listen, the police were questioning me for hours, trying to convince me to testify against Stefan but obviously I said nothing. They were making threats about my being an accomplice but eventually they let me go. They've told me not to leave Brighton."

"Make sure you don't say anything," Victor warned. "Stefan and Dimitry will keep quiet so the police won't have anything on me."

"What will you do, Victor?"

"I'm not sure. I'll be in touch."

As soon as the call was ended, she dialled a sleepy sounding Afina. "I just heard from Victor."

"What do you mean, you heard from Victor?" Afina replied suddenly very awake.

"He telephoned me and I had to tell him about Stefan and Dimitry. I didn't mention Powell but he knows where to find you both and I think he blames you both for everything."

Afina was obviously shocked. "Did he say what he is going to do?"

"No. On the positive side, he trusts me so if I hear from him again I will warn you."

"Is he coming to Brighton?"

"He didn't say."

"I need to tell Powell. Please call me if you hear from him again."

"Of course I will and don't worry. Powell dealt with Victor before and I'm sure he can again if necessary."

Afina didn't share Mara's confidence but thanked her and went to find Powell.

Mara returned to the bedroom to find Emma awake. "Sorry," she apologised.

"You woke me up," Emma complained. "Now you're going to have to help me get back to sleep."

"And how exactly do I do that?"

"I'll leave that up to you but if you need a clue, I can tell you I usually sleep very well after I've had at least two orgasms."

"Greedy girl," Mara said and jumped on the bed.

CHAPTER FORTY

Afina was surprised Powell already knew that Victor was free but had said nothing. She recounted the details of her phone call with Mara while he prepared a late breakfast of coffee and rolls.

"I doubt he will come to Brighton," Powell said. "And if he does it's likely he will contact Mara again, so we should get a warning he's on his way. I don't think we need to be too concerned." He didn't want Afina spending every waking minute terrified by the thought of the imminent arrival of Victor.

"But he knows who you are."

"There are two police officers in a car outside but remember Victor doesn't actually know where I live, he only knows the bar. There are also two officers on his tail since he left the hospital this morning. If he has any sense, he'll be on the first flight out of here."

"I thought you had dealt with him," Afina said accusingly. Then realising she had been unfair added, "Sorry, without you he probably would have killed me."

"That's okay. It was only ever a temporary solution but I didn't expect him to be free this soon."

"What are we going to do?"

"We need to book some flights to get the other girls back home. What about your mother and sister?"

"Mama is still desperate to go home. She is worried about losing her job if she spends any more time away."

"What about Adriana? Would she perhaps like to stay a bit longer?"

"She loves it here so I'm sure she'd be happy to stay."

"Okay, so we let your mother go home and Adriana stays here. After a couple of weeks we can decide whether we feel it's safe for Adriana to leave or not. Do you think your mother would be prepared to move apartment, preferably to a different city?

"I don't know. Work is difficult to find and she has a job so I'm not sure she could move city but maybe apartment."

"You speak with her and see what she says. I'll book flights for the others."

Victor came off the phone to Mara knowing he must visit Brighton. He would not be made a fool of by anyone. Neither was he the type of man to desert his friends and he had no intention of running scared back to Bucharest. He would make Powell and Afina pay for what they had done. He would be sure to have a lot of fun with Afina before he left her, not dead, but so broken she would never be the same again. Powell was dangerous and he would have to kill him.

Right now though he had a problem because he was sure he was being followed. He had taken a taxi from the hospital to Portsmouth and found a café serving breakfast. While calling Mara he had noticed two men enter and order coffee. They looked out of place in the café. They were wearing suits and ties, unlike the other customers who were far more working class. After he finished his breakfast he led them towards various shops and using the glass windows as mirrors, he was able to spot them again, lurking in the background.

Victor pretended to be interested in buying some clothes, visiting several shops until he found the right one. It was on the ground floor of the shopping centre and the third time he had tried on some trousers, only this time he didn't bother actually putting them on. The layout of the changing rooms meant he was out of sight from anyone in the shop and the door through which he'd seen an assistant enter would almost certainly lead to a rear exit. After a few minutes, he returned to the shop floor and took a further pair of the trousers from the shelf, explaining loudly to the assistant he had put on more weight than he realised and needed a bigger size.

He ambled back to the changing room just as a shop assistant punched in the number on the keypad, allowing her to exit. Victor had no trouble identifying the assistant had entered 0101. A few seconds later he punched in the numbers and he was thankful the door opened.

Once through the door he looked around and realised he was in a stock room. The young girl he had followed through the door was taking something down from a shelf. He walked swiftly towards her and she turned towards him with a look of surprise on her face as she saw it was someone unfamiliar. Victor threw a punch that caught her squarely on the chin and sent her flying backwards. He bent over her and put his large hand around her small throat. She was bleeding from a cut lip.

"Don't make any noise," he warned. "Do you have a car?"

"Yes," the girl answered, obviously terrified. "It's out back."

"Give me the keys."

"They're in my jacket, hanging over there on the wall."

Victor dragged her to her feet and hurried her towards where she'd pointed. He never loosened his grip as she took some keys from her coat pocket and handed them to him. He then dragged her towards the rear door and tried entering 0101 again on the keypad but nothing happened.

"What's the number?" he demanded, squeezing the girl's throat a little harder.

"Four, three, four, three."

He punched in the number and emerged onto an access road with large dustbins and a few parked cars. There was nobody else around. "Which is yours?"

"The Mondeo," she said, pointing at her car.

He pushed the electronic unlock button and the lights of the Mondeo briefly flashed. He half dragged her to the driver's side of the car. "Get in," he said, pushing her on to the back seat. "Lie there and keep quiet, and you won't get hurt."

He jumped in the driver's seat and sped away. After a couple of miles he was sure he wasn't being followed but he knew he had to ditch the car. The police would already have a description out for the car and the girl. He drove past a taxi rank and decided it was time to change vehicles.

"In the minute I'm going to stop and you are going to get in the front of the car and drive away as fast and as far as you can. Do you understand me?"

There was no response from the back seat. "Do you understand me," he repeated louder and more threateningly.

"Yes," came a timid reply.

"What's your name?"

"Phoebe."

"Well Phoebe, if you keep driving for at least twenty minutes I won't have to come looking for you. You don't want me to come looking for you, do you?"

"No."

"Okay, so get ready, I'm going to get out in just a minute."

He made a couple of turns and headed back towards the taxis. He pulled into the side of the road, jumped out and gripping the arm of the girl pushed her into the driver's seat. "Now drive for twenty minutes," he shouted and slammed the car door.

She drove away without needing any further encouragement and he walked briskly to the first taxi. The police would have no trouble following his immediate trail but he had sufficient head start and they would soon hit a dead end.

"The station, please," he instructed the taxi driver once seated. "And I'm in a hurry."

CHAPTER FORTY ONE

Mara finally returned to Stefan's house in the afternoon. She had enjoyed her time with Emma and Rebecca but needed to change clothes as much as anything and all her worldly possessions were in the house. She also had nowhere else to stay as she wasn't willing to waste money on a hotel, when she had a free room at the house. Neither could she expect to stay with the girls. They were a very happy couple and she was strictly a toy for them to enjoy sharing, which suited her fine as she had no wish for any further complications in her life.

As she entered the house she felt strange knowing for the first time ever she would be the only person in the house. Out of curiosity, she went up the stairs to Stefan's room and though she wasn't sure what she expected to see different, she was surprised it all seemed very normal, except of course Stefan was in prison. There was half a sandwich on a plate and a cold mug of tea, suggesting he was probably eating when the police stormed the building. She had been downstairs in her room and the police had taken her away before she knew exactly what had happened to Stefan. He had probably not resisted. There would have been little he could do against several burly police officers.

She turned to go back to her room and stood rooted to the spot when she saw Victor standing in the doorway.

"I've been waiting for you," Victor said. "I was beginning to wonder if you were ever coming back."

"We can't be having any punters back here at the moment so I was just out and about." She tried not to show the nervousness she was feeling. "I think I'm going to go home for a visit until things here are sorted out."

"Probably a good idea. I need to think about how I can help Dimitry and Stefan before finding a new house to operate from, then you can start working again."

"So where have you been?" Mara asked. "Stefan and Dimitry were really worried about you."

Victor walked into the room, approached the sink and filled the kettle.

"Cup of tea?" he asked.

"No thanks." Mara didn't want to spend time in his company.

"Afina tricked me and I ended up in a bloody hospital for crazy people," he said, putting a teabag in a cup. He poured water from the kettle and added some milk from the fridge, then he carried his finished cup of tea back into the lounge. "Look how English I am becoming," he laughed. "Before I came to this country I never drank tea." He took a sip and looked Mara in the eye. "I just have one question for you, Mara. How do you know Powell?"

Mara was taken aback by the question. Her mind was racing, trying to calculate what she could safely say. "What do you mean?" she replied, stalling for time.

"On the phone, when I blamed Powell for my troubles, you asked why I blamed him. It took me a second to realise you shouldn't have heard of Powell. So I repeat my question, how do you know Powell?"

Mara couldn't believe she had been so stupid but she'd been shagged out and nursing a hangover so she hadn't been exactly thinking clearly. "Powell was a punter here. I saw him once but then he became a regular of Afina's. I didn't understand what he had to do with anything."

"He was a regular customer of Afina? That explains a lot. He was also the father of that young police officer Dimitry stabbed. He must have been trying to find out what happened and was working with Afina for revenge."

"The police officer's father!" Mara appeared shocked. "Shit!" She was amazed how good an actress she had become. Then again all those fake orgasms showed she could act.

"Have you spoken with Stefan?" Victor asked.

"No. I don't even know where they have him or how to contact him."

"Okay. I'm going to have my tea and think. I need to decide what to do next. You can go to your room."

"Let me know if I can help," Mara offered and then quickly left. She let out a huge sigh of relief once back in her room.

As she sat on her bed, she realised it was probably only a matter of time before Victor spoke with either Stefan or Dimitry and learned Powell and Danny were the same person. Then the shit would truly hit the fan and he would know she knew more than she was telling.

Next she thought about what Victor had said about finding a new house where they could carry on working. Stefan didn't actually own the building where she was living, he had rented it. Victor and the others back home would want to quickly get the business back on its feet. They wouldn't want to go too long without the lucrative income they made. They would probably look to send someone new to carry on the business but that wasn't necessary. She was already here and understood the business better than any newcomer could. She felt like she had been hit with a bolt of lightning. She'd spent enough time on her back earning a living. Maybe there was a better way to make money from the efforts of other working girls. She would make some phone calls.

CHAPTER FORTY TWO

Powell started the day by driving Afina, plus her mother and sister, to Gatwick airport. Lia, Cosmina and Violette were in a separate taxi, which Powell was following. Afina and Adriana weren't going to be catching a plane but the rest were all on their way back to Bucharest and Powell was pleased he had been able to help them return home safely. He was also happy his home would no longer feel like he was running a bed and breakfast. In a very short space of time he had gone from living alone to sharing with six females who were almost total strangers. It was an experience he was unlikely to ever forget.

The round trip took a couple of hours and once back at the house, Afina and Adriana packed their possessions into the back of Powell's car and he drove them to the bar. Until recent events he would have said he was driving them to Bella's but he had stopped calling the bar by its name. He couldn't imagine ever renaming the place but for the time being it would be known just simply as the bar.

He'd been annoyed when he heard Victor had disappeared. It almost certainly suggested he had no intention of going away and it was highly possible he was going to be further trouble. He could have returned to Brighton but Mara hadn't seen him, although it was possible he was laying low in one of the many small hotels. Equally, he may be hiding out with another of his customers for girls in some other part of the country. Powell knew he wouldn't be able to rest until Victor was located.

Brian had told him the police were trying to get Stefan to reveal more about his operation in return for a lighter sentence but he was saying nothing. The girls Powell had rescued had all made statements, which meant Stefan was facing a very lengthy time in prison but he had hardly said a word since being arrested.

Powell left the girls to unpack and spent some time catching up on admin for the bar. He was pleased to see Neil was doing a decent job with managing stock and takings were at the normal level so perhaps he really wasn't needed. If that was the case, he might look to change career. He needed some new motivation in his life, which the bar could no longer provide. He had proved recently that the skills he had acquired over many years could be put to better use than just pulling pints. It was certainly something to consider but the immediate issue was still locating and nullifying Victor.

Mara had received a quite positive reaction to the suggestion she made, which she had summarised as being the best option for returning to business as usual, in the shortest possible time. She should be considered a straight swap for Stefan, and then the money would soon start to flow again. She had worked alongside Stefan for two years and knew all the contacts, customers and methods of doing business.

Twenty four hours after placing the first call to her Uncle, she received approval to take over from Stefan for three months on a trial basis. She was elated and had been given some immediate tasks. The three girls who were supposed to be arriving for Danny's imaginary business were ready to travel plus one other girl. Mara needed to find a new temporary property and arrange with Danny to have them collected immediately after their arrival in Brighton. They wanted all that to happen within a week.

Someone called Radu was travelling with the girls and would become Mara's muscle. It had been agreed she and Radu should select one of the girls to start working immediately from the new property and the other three would go to Danny.

Mara knew these arrangements presented a significant problem. There was no such person as Danny and Powell would not be paying for any girls. There was also a secondary problem, which was that Radu would no doubt be reporting back on her and may even be destined to take over from her, after he became familiar with the business, if she messed up.

Unlike Afina, Mara could not simply run away from everything. The organisation would hunt her down and she had too much family back home, who she would be putting in danger. She was beginning to regret her ambition. She should have just told Powell that Victor was back at the house and asked him to sort the problem. After all, it was Powell who had caused most of the problems she was now facing. She needed a way of getting rid of Victor and explaining away Danny no longer wanting the girls. Maybe, just maybe she had the inkling of an idea.

Her thoughts were interrupted by Victor knocking on the door to her room. He had taken to regularly coming downstairs for a coffee as he was feeling bored. He was wisely not risking going out and getting spotted. She opened the door and the smell of whisky on his breath hit her in the face as he walked into the room without waiting for an invite.

"I finally tracked down that bloody solicitor," Victor announced. "He says Stefan is on remand and can have three visits of one hour a week until he goes to trial."

"Are you going to go see him?" Mara asked, hiding her concern.

"Of course I'm not fucking going," he swore. "The police are looking for me."

"I could go," Mara suggested.

She was pleased Powell had confirmed her life was once again private as he was no longer listening to what was being broadcast from her bedroom. She would return the small transmitter to him the next time she saw Afina. Until then, she had taken the precaution of placing it in a drawer covered with clothes, just in case he changed his mind and decided to have a listen.

"That would probably be best," Victor agreed. "Speak to the solicitor and arrange a visit for as soon as possible."

"What do you want me to say to Stefan?"

"We can discuss that later. Right now I'm feeling horny."

Mara had thought it inevitable he would eventually expect sex and she knew he sure as hell wouldn't take no for an answer, so she had no choice in the matter.

She put on her acting face, smiled and came close to him. She slithered down his body to her knees and extracted his semi rigid cock. This is the last bloody time I'm doing this for him, or anyone not of my choosing, she was thinking as she took him in her mouth.

CHAPTER FORTY THREE

Afina had worked her first full evening shift in the bar. She felt good about doing an honest job and had enjoyed the interaction with people. She had waited on the tables until they stopped serving food and then spent some time behind the bar learning how to pour a pint of beer. After a bit of practice she was able to pour a pint without too much froth getting in the way.

Powell had spent most of the evening just chatting to customers and making sure everything ran smoothly but more than once she turned in his direction and noticed him watching her. He just gave her an encouraging smile each time. Perhaps he was just checking on his new member of staff. She was uncertain what Powell was truly feeling. She was hugely grateful to him and she found him attractive despite the age difference but she was worried his interest was more paternal and linked to the loss of his daughter. Still, now she was staying in Brighton, there was no rush to complicate their relationship with anything more than friendship, at least for the time being.

Afina's mother was home safe and Adriana had spent the evening upstairs watching television, trying to improve her English. Powell had left Neil to lock up and headed home after laughing with Afina about how empty his house would feel with everybody finally gone. Afina realised just how tired she was feeling but she was also buzzing with a sense of excitement. She didn't want to go straight to bed despite it being after Midnight. The only person she knew who would probably still be awake was Mara so she sent her a text asking if she wanted to meet for a drink.

The response was almost immediate and Mara suggested meeting at the bar Emma and Becky had first taken her, which was always open to three in the morning. They both agreed to meet in twenty minutes at the bar.

Afina arrived first but it was only five minutes later she spotted Mara entering. Afina was at the bar buying a bottle of Pinot Grigio for them to share. It was a quiet evening and they easily found a table with a couple of seats. Most people seemed to prefer to stand so they could easily circulate and meet people. A couple of girls smiled at Afina in recognition but the presence of Mara kept them at bay.

"How are you?" Afina asked.

"The better for seeing you?" Mara replied, with a mischievous smile.

"Are you flirting with me?"

"Maybe!"

"Keep your flirting for Emma and Becky," Afina suggested.

"We are well past flirting."

"I'm sure you are," Afina laughed. "Anyway, it is good to see you. Have you heard again from Victor?"

"No, I would have told you if I had. No news is good news. It probably means he is back in Bucharest."

"Yes, probably," Afina agreed.

"So tell me all your news. Have you been fucking Powell?"

"Mara, you are terrible… And no I haven't."

"So you've been saving yourself for me," Mara joked.

"Maybe," Afina teased.

"I think I need to get you drunk!"

"You can try."

Victor had watched Mara enter the bar and was about to follow her in when he noticed the rainbow badge on the door, which signalled it was a gay bar. He had learned the significance of the badge when first coming to Brighton and on a couple of occasions stumbling into a bar, which it quickly became clear was full of gays. Eventually someone had explained the significance of the rainbow badge outside. Now he avoided such places like the plague. He liked to watch two girls playing with each other but the idea of guys was disgusting. If a gay guy tied to hit on him, Victor knew he would beat him to a pulp so it was just better to avoid the gay bars and not risk getting into trouble with the police.

When he'd heard her leaving the house, he'd wondered where she was going so late at night and on an impulse decided to follow her. It had only been a ten minute walk to the bar but he was ready for a drink by the time he arrived. He was surprised Mara should want to visit a gay bar. He was quite certain she wasn't gay. No one could give blowjobs the way she did and be gay. Was she meeting someone and if so who? Maybe it would be someone who would be up for a threesum. Gay bar or not he needed to take a look inside.

He opened the door and entered, immediately noticing the absence of any men. He felt a bit conspicuous as he glanced around and spotted Mara sitting with Afina drinking wine and laughing. He quickly turned around and left the bar, hardly able to believe what he'd seen. Mara was with that bitch Afina! Maybe they were both gay, or perhaps it was just a convenient place to meet. Whatever the reason, he'd just got very lucky.

He moved further away down the street from the bar, where he still had a good view of anyone leaving but he wasn't so easily seen. He was grinning at the thought of what lay ahead. He was surprised the stupid bitch hadn't left the country. He knew where to find Powell and was willing to wait for his revenge but it had been Afina who led him to Powell and he intended to make her pay for the grief she had caused.

Mara wouldn't take Afina back to the house because he was there so they would have to go somewhere else. For some reason he assumed they would be going somewhere, either to screw or to keep drinking. If he was wrong and they said goodbye at the door it would be more difficult. If Afina was staying at the bar she wouldn't be walking home, it was too far, so she would be taking a taxi, in which case it was a five minute walk to the nearest taxi rank. He patted his inside jacket pocket and was reminded there was no blade. He felt naked going out without a knife but he hadn't yet had the opportunity to pick one up since returning to Brighton.

In fact, he was going to need more than just a knife when it came to confronting Powell. He knew just the person to call. Mike had lost one of his best brothels in Leeds thanks to Powell's actions. If Victor let him know who was responsible and where to find the culprit he was sure to seek revenge. When he returned to the house he would call Mike and make some arrangements. Mike would be able to provide men and guns. They knew each other quite well and would make a good team. Powell didn't have a chance.

Victor turned his mind back to Afina. He had no interest in just killing Afina. That would be far too easy. He intended to make her pay and just the thought of those pleasures was enough to make his cock start to stir. It was going to be difficult to grab her off the street, there were too many people about and he had no weapon. He was undecided what to do and he had to be careful. If he fell into police hands he wasn't going to be able to get away again so easily.

He decided he had to be patient and choose the right moment for taking care of Afina. If she hadn't left Brighton after everything that had happened so far, then it was a pretty safe bet she was planning on staying. Perhaps Mara was the reason she was still here. He was confident he would be able to get to Afina through Mara, when the time was right.

He would also have to keep a close eye on Mara. She had already admitted to knowing Powell but the way she told it, she had only had sex with him once and then he had moved on to Afina. Why he would choose to have the skinny, pale skinned Afina rather than Mara was beyond his comprehension but hell, every man had different tastes in girls. He would have to confront Mara but tonight was not the right time so he turned away and walked back to the house.

CHAPTER FORTY FOUR

Mara's prison visit to Stefan had been organised for eleven. She arrived early at Lewes prison and was put through a thorough search procedure before being admitted to meet with him.

"Hello Stefan," she greeted him, sat in one of the two chairs at the small metal table. There was just one guard in uniform standing at the side of the room.

"Good to see you, Mara."

"How is it?" she asked.

"Quite reasonable actually. Nothing like our jails back home. This is a picnic by comparison. Good food and I even have a television."

"It's all Victor's fault. He called me and wants me to work in his new business. Can you believe his nerve! He also boasted he was responsible for getting rid of you and Dimitry."

"If Victor is branching out on his own then he must have some support back home from powerful people. You need to be careful."

"I've spoken with the people in Bucharest and they want me to take over the business, at least for the time being. I need to urgently find a new property in Brighton as they have some girls ready to travel."

"Are you sure you want to get so involved? It could be dangerous. Why don't you take your money and go back home?"

"And what do I do when I get there? I like being in England and making money. This is my chance to get off my back and make some money through other girls."

"I guess that's true but Victor might try to stop you. Have you told anyone back home Victor is responsible for this mess?"

"Not yet."

"Do so as soon as possible and get some muscle sent to help you."

"They are sending someone with the girls next week."

"Good. Listen, have you heard from Danny?"

"No I haven't. Do you think he's been arrested?"

"I have no idea but he had two girls he was delivering for me and I was even beginning to wonder if he had something to do with this mess."

"I need to get hold of him because they want to send his girls over next week and he will need to pay for them."

"Damn! I don't know his number. I had it in my phone and the police have it. He probably tried calling me."

"Perhaps he'll come by the house once he thinks it's safe."

"I hope so. He gave us fifty thousand pounds so I can't imagine he will just forget about the money."

Mara's brain was suddenly racing. She was shocked to discover Powell had given Stefan fifty thousand pounds. Was he really that rich he could afford to toss away so much money? No wonder Stefan had welcomed him with open arms. "If he does turn up to collect the girls how does he pay for them?"

"By bank transfer, like before. He has the account details and soon as you see the money's in the account, you can let him take the girls."

"How will I know if the money is in the account?"

Stefan thought about her question for a moment. "I forgot you don't have access to my account." He leaned slightly closer. "Do you remember our mothers' maiden names?"

"Of course."

"I have an email account of my middle name, dot our mothers' maiden name, at gmail dot com. The password is Corina followed by the month of my birthday. Every other letter is a capital."

"Corina? I didn't know you liked her music." Mara didn't like her music despite her being very popular back home.

"Well I do. Now, have you got all that?"

"Yes."

"So if you go into my account you will find a folder called UBS which has my account details. My password is the same for the account as I just gave you."

Mara recited the details again in her mind. "Okay, I've got that."

"If you hear from Danny, don't give him the girls until the money is in the account. Do you understand?"

"I'm not stupid."

"No you're not. Make sure you are tough with the new girls."

"Don't worry, I know what I'm doing. I'll come visit you again next week and let you know how it's going."

"Thanks Mara. At the end of the day family is everything."

"Only when it suits you, Stefan."

"What do you mean?"

"You have a short memory! Not long ago you were letting Dimitry and Danny do what they want with me."

"I told them not to go too far. That was because we are family."

"Thanks for nothing!"

Mara was deep in thought as she left the prison and headed back to Brighton in the back of a taxi. She was desperate to take a look at Stefan's bank account and check the balance. It was a dangerous game to play but it might be worth it, if the account held a healthy balance.

CHAPTER FORTY FIVE

"So did you tell Stefan about Powell?" Victor asked, as soon as Mara returned to the house.

"Of course I did," Mara answered. "He was shocked but said to do nothing for the time being. He doesn't want you ending up in jail as well. He suggests you get the next plane home."

"I'm going nowhere, at least not until I deal with that bitch Afina."

"Well I'm sure she's already back in Bucharest."

"Maybe but maybe not."

"I have work to do," Mara said dismissively.

She returned downstairs to her room and went straight to her laptop. Within a couple of minutes she had followed Stefan's instructions and found herself staring at his bank account details. The balance was over two hundred thousand pounds. She looked at recent statements and identified that as payments went into the account, amounts equivalent to ninety per cent were immediately transferred out of the account. Her cousin was a very rich man even with his ten per cent share.

Mara felt a pang of jealousy. While she was offering her arse to anyone and everyone, her cousin was sitting on his arse banking loads of money. It was not an equitable arrangement.

She signed out of the account and spent some time thinking about her options. She had to urgently deal with Victor, which was easier said than done. He was the only obstacle to a better future and also a threat to her life. It was quite appealing to simply transfer the money to her account, go straight to the airport and get on a plane to somewhere very far away but they would hunt her down and she didn't fancy spending the rest of her life looking over her shoulder and unable to return home.

Though the money would be nice, she was equally attracted to the opportunity of taking over from Stefan. She would be able to make a great deal of money over the next few years if Stefan's bank balance was an indication of what she could expect. She would also earn the respect of the people back home. There weren't any other women in the organisation trusted with real responsibility.

On balance the second option seemed best because it had the added attraction of being able to stay in Brighton and she still harboured the hope that one day she might succeed in seducing Afina. She wasn't sure why it was but that damn girl had really messed with her head.

Mara telephoned Bucharest and informed them she had heard from Danny and he didn't want the girls. He was doubting whether he had picked the right people as partners, given the recent arrests and publicity it created. He wanted to wait a month until the furore died down and then he would be back in contact. Although they weren't happy at the other end of the phone, they did seem to have some sympathy for his view and they still had his deposit. Mara was told to hurry up with finding the new property and the new girls could then be put to work locally so she decided to spend the afternoon visiting agents.

Much as she didn't like Victor, she had to admit he had his uses, he was especially good at getting new girls quickly under control, something she was going to find difficult without Dimitry's large cock or Victor's penchant for delivering a beating. She found Victor upstairs and told him she wouldn't be around in the evening as she was going out with friends. As he was permanently stuck in the house, she got a kind of perverse pleasure from telling him not to expect her back. She knew she would get an invite back to Emma and Becky's but there was also the small possibility she would be able to spend the night with Afina.

She had one last task to accomplish before she left for the evening. There had been an idea knocking about in her head all day and on a sudden impulse she decided it would be a good idea to do it before leaving and before she changed her mind. As she went outside to her taxi, she was feeling happy about her action and life in general.

Powell was surprised by how quickly Afina grasped everything about bar work. She worked hard and always smiled like she was really enjoying her work. Everyone liked working with her and the customers also approved. He struggled with the fact he found himself attracted to her despite the large age gap. What made the attraction stranger was that over the last twenty years there had been very few times he'd felt anything similar. For many years, he shut out his emotions and just dedicated himself to the memory of Vanessa and bringing up Bella. There had been some brief physical relationships but no one had really connected with him on an emotional level. So how someone so young could have such an impact was baffling. It could only be a midlife crisis brought on by the loss of Bella.

What he definitely didn't want was to hurt Afina. She had been hurt enough. He felt he had little to offer her in the way of a future. One day she would want children and in time her crush on him would fade away and it could only end badly. Yet still there was an indisputable attraction, which wasn't lessened by the fact he had enjoyed having sex with her. Every so often he would be looking at her in the bar and a picture would invade his mind, reminding him of the time they had spent together, and no matter how hard he tried to dismiss it, would act as an unwelcome stimulation to his body. At least those occasions were proof he was still very much alive.

There had been no sightings of Victor and Powell was beginning to think he had indeed left the country or at the very least was staying clear of Brighton. Maybe Victor did have some brains to go with all that brawn.

The return to something like normality had a negative aspect, it left him with more time to think and dwell on the loss of the two people he had truly loved in his life. He hadn't had any nightmares about Vanessa or Bella for several days but found himself during the daytime talking to them in his head, asking their opinions as if they were there with him. What should he do with Afina? Should he sell the bar? The questions were endless.

It was confirmation he needed a new direction in life and he was starting to formulate an idea. It would not be a commercially motivated venture like the bar but something that was good for his soul. He needed to throw his energy into something worthwhile and reading the local paper had given him an idea. It was potentially dangerous but very emotionally rewarding.

Afina had the night off work and she had invited Powell to meet up with her friends and Adriana, to go for a meal in the Marina. Adriana, Mara, Emma and Becky would be going so he was once again going to be badly outnumbered as the only man present.

Afina had asked his advice on where to eat and he had suggested a recently opened Indian restaurant, which Bella had visited and recommended to him. He took a taxi to the bar, picking up Afina and Adriana, before continuing to the Marina. They were first to arrive and seated at a circular table, Powell ordered a bottle of inexpensive, pink Cava.

"Would you like some?" he asked Adriana.

She shot a nervous glance at Afina as she said, "Yes please."

Afina smiled and said, "Just the one glass."

The others arrived soon after and a second bottle of Cava was quickly ordered. Afina and Adriana had never eaten Indian food before so left Powell to choose, with the proviso it wasn't too spicy. The restaurant was quite busy and they sat eating Poppadoms and drinking Cava, waiting for their starters to arrive. Powell looked around at the smiling faces and he once again felt the pain of loss for Bella, which was exacerbated by how his young companions were so alive and vibrant.

Powell was so focused on his thoughts, he didn't notice the two men approaching the table until they were only six feet away. A sixth sense made him look up just in time to see the first man lift his arm up and point the gun in his direction.

He moved with lightning reflexes, honed by years of kickboxing training and grabbing the edge of the table lifted it like a shield and found it was light enough to propel in the general direction of both men. As the cutlery and glasses crashed to the floor, everyone at the table cried out in shock at what Powell had done, but in the same instant heard the sound of gunshots as the first man fired twice fired wildly before the table collided with his raised arms and the gun fell to the floor.

Both men staggered backwards under the weight of the table and the girls were screaming as they tried to run from their seats, heading in all directions, desperately trying to escape. The other customers reacted similarly and chaos ensued. The table was upside down on the floor with its legs sticking in the air. Powell leaped across the space previously occupied by the table and aimed a kick at one man's groin, which doubled him up in severe pain and caused his weapon to fall noisily to the ground. The other man was trying to retrieve his gun from the floor where it had skidded under the next table.

Powell nimbly advanced and just as the man stood up, once again holding the gun, Powell kicked him and connected with the wrist holding the gun, deflecting the man's aim and sending a bullet harmlessly into the ceiling. Powell was immediately spinning and lashing out in the direction of the man's chin, sending him hurtling to the floor.

The other man was recovering from the kick to his groin and reaching down to his leg, took hold of a menacing looking knife, which had been strapped to the outside of his lower leg.

Powell warily advanced towards the man. He was determined to engage both men at least long enough for everyone else to escape and he was succeeding, as the restaurant was fast emptying.

I'll fucking cut you in two," the man threatened and lunged towards Powell, who easily stepped inside and grabbed the man's wrist. He stretched the arm and bent it backwards, causing the man to drop his knife and scream in agony.

Powell used his legs to sweep the man's legs away and send him to the ground. Powell maintained a hold on his wrist and the weight of his body falling caused his arm to snap. Powell kicked him flush on the chin, silencing the piercing scream he'd started to emit, leaving him unmoving on the ground.

The other man was still out cold on the floor. Powell had time to glance around the restaurant and saw some diners were cowering at one end of the restaurant behind the bar area. He could see no sign of the girls. They must have escaped outside.

"Has someone called the police," Powell asked out loud.

"Yes," the Indian waiter who had served them responded. "They are on their way."

"Good. You can all relax," Powell said.

He saw people cautiously emerging from behind the bar as he was picking up both guns from the floor and covered the two men. A minute later he heard the sound of police sirens converging on the restaurant.

CHAPTER FORTY SIX

When Powell suddenly threw the table at the two attackers, Afina had instantly understood their lives were in danger and her first concern had been to get Adriana to safety. As the mayhem erupted, Afina grabbed Adriana by the hand and pulled her towards the entrance to the restaurant. Keeping low she could see many others heading in the same direction but her only focus was Adriana.

Once on the pavement outside she looked back through the glass windows of the restaurant to see Powell kicking one of the assailants. The other was already on the ground and Afina breathed a sigh of relief Powell was alive and looking in control of the situation. Everyone else emerging from the restaurant continued to run down the street trying to get as far away as possible from the source of danger. She could see no sign of the other girls and assumed they also had put distance between themselves and the gunmen.

In the swirl of bodies Afina didn't at first realise someone was next to her and pushing something into her ribs.

"Hello Afina," Victor said. "Don't move, this is a gun you can feel not my cock."

Afina turned towards the voice she recognised and hated. "What do you want?"

"You're coming with me. Get rid of the friend and let's go." He dug the gun into her side. "No messing or I'll just shoot you here."

"Adriana, run down the road and find the others. I'm going to wait here for Powell." She was so pleased Victor didn't know Adriana was her sister. Afina doubted he would let her go if he knew of their relationship. Sensing reluctance on Adriana's part, Afina raised her voice, "Go now," she commanded.

As Adriana ran down the road, Victor gripped Afina's arm and led her in the opposite direction. All the time he had the gun hidden beneath the coat over his arm sticking into Afina's side. He led her up some steps and along a busy walkway fronting the sea.

"It looks like Powell has more lives than a cat," Victor said. "But he won't keep getting lucky."

"Where are we going?" Afina asked.

"Back home, of course," he answered. "I've missed you."

"Afina was surprised they were heading for the house and took a crumb of comfort from the fact she knew where she was going. Surely it would be the first place Powell would look for her. Perhaps that was even what Victor wanted, to lure him to the house. Perhaps she was the bait in the trap. At least everyone else was safe and in particular Adriana.

There were restaurants to her right and after just a couple of minutes they were in the Marina car park. Victor led the way up two floors and strode to an old Volvo. He opened the passenger door and pushed her inside.

"Don't cause me any trouble," he threatened. "I will shoot you and anyone else who gets in my way."

Afina sat obediently in the seat while Victor hurried around to the driver's side and sat beside her. He turned the key and reversed out the space. Within five minutes they were driving into the centre of Brighton. He turned right after about a mile and parked in a further underground car park bearing the name Regency Square.

He pulled her from the car and they ascended some steps to emerge only a couple of streets from the house where she had hoped and expected never to return.

When armed police arrived at the restaurant, Powell was instructed to lie on the floor with his hands behind his back and he did as asked. It took only a few minutes for the explanations which led to the police being satisfied he was an innocent victim not a perpetrator of any crime. He was keen to find the girls but wasn't unduly worried as there had been no casualties and they had all done the sensible thing by running away.

When the officer in charge understood he was Bella's father he had many questions about why he was being targeted by two killers. Powell gave him a very brief explanation of recent events but pointed him to Chief Inspector Brown for corroboration.

After ten minutes and realising the questions were going to go on for quite a bit longer he called Afina's number but there was no answer. He had been talking to the police for almost thirty minutes when he saw Adriana,

Emma and Rebecca at the entrance to the restaurant. They seemed anxious but a broad shouldered police officer was stopping them from entering. Powell walked across to join them.

"These are my friends," Powell explained to the police officer. "They were sat with me so are all witnesses and I'm sure the man in charge will want to interview them."

"Powell, we can't find Afina," Emma shouted to him in a worried voice and barged past the police officer. The others followed suit and the officer gave into the unequal struggle and let them enter.

Adriana added, "She led me outside to safety but then she sent me to find the others while she stayed behind."

"Maybe she is somewhere looking for you guys right now," Powell said far calmer than he was feeling inside.

"She's not answering her phone," Becky said.

"Where's Mara?" Powell asked. "Could they be together?"

Emma answered, "Mara took a taxi home before we walked back to the restaurant. We all thought Afina would be waiting here for us."

"Could you girls do me a huge favour and take Adriana back to the bar and I'll continue looking for Afina. I'm sure she'll turn up shortly."

"Wouldn't it be better if we all looked for her?" Becky asked.

There was a certain logic to Becky's suggestion but Powell wanted them all as far away as possible, in case of further trouble. He couldn't properly look for Afina while at the same time having to babysit three other girls. "The police are going to want to interview you all. You are key witnesses as you were sat with me. When they've finished they might offer a lift back to Brighton but if not then grab a taxi. Keep phoning Afina and let me know if you hear anything."

"So you are worried something's happened to her?" Becky pressed.

"It's unlikely but there could have been more men waiting outside the restaurant. Please just do as I ask and we'll speak a bit later. I'll introduce you to the police officer in charge and explain about Afina, then I'll go looking for her."

"Make sure you call us as soon as you know anything," Emma stressed.

"Will do." Powell promised.

CHAPTER FORTY SEVEN

Mara was disappointed how the evening had turned out. There had been no dinner, followed by a near death experience and then the girls had said they didn't feel like partying so Mara had taken a taxi home alone. She couldn't be certain but was wondering if Victor was responsible for the attack at the restaurant. Powell didn't seem like the type of guy to collect more than one enemy wanting him dead.

She opened her front door and as she entered, shouted up the stairs, "Victor, you at home?"

"I'm up here," came the reply.

Mara marched up the stairs in a determined mood. She was fed up with Victor and he was putting the whole business at risk with his thirst for revenge.

She entered Stefan's living room and Victor was waiting for her with a huge smile on his face. "So glad you could join us," he said.

It took a second for what he had said to sink in. "Aren't you alone?"

"No I'm not. An old friend of yours has come to pay us a visit."

Mara wondered if Stefan or Dimitry had somehow escaped from prison. "Where is this friend?" she asked.

"Come and see," Victor replied and led the way to the bedroom.

Mara was shocked to see a naked Afina lying face down on the bed, her wrists and ankles shackled to the four corners of the bed. She turned her head in the direction of Mara when she heard her enter the room but couldn't speak as she had tape across her mouth. Mara hurried to the side of the bed and was relieved to see Afina looked alive and well. She stroked Afina's forehead and gave a smile of encouragement.

"Just like old times," Victor quipped but no one laughed.

"Are you alright," Mara asked Afina, who nodded affirmatively as a reply.

"Of course she's alright, we haven't started yet. I wasn't expecting you back, Mara, but now you're here I might as well let you expend all your energy while I play Director."

"Director?"

"Did I not say? I'm planning to make a short film. Not for the mass market but something her friend Powell will appreciate."

Mara was wishing she hadn't come home. "I don't want to be part of any film," Mara stated firmly. "I suppose it was you organised for those gunmen to try and kill Powell at the restaurant?"

"Yes and I haven't said thank you for leading us to the restaurant. We couldn't have done it without you."

Mara didn't like hearing of her part in the evening's events. So Victor had followed her, which meant he knew she was somehow implicated with Afina and Powell. She had to be very careful what she said and did. "What are you going to do?"

"As I said, it's just like old times." He undid the belt to his trousers and pulled it free. It was made of leather and had a large metal buckle. "We don't need any fancy toys today, this will do fine."

"I don't want any fucking part of this," Mara swore. "You're a bloody fool. It won't take long for Powell to realise Afina is missing and you're responsible. This house will be flooded with police within the hour."

"Then we better get a move on."

"Mara's phone rang with a number she didn't recognise. "Hello," she answered tentatively.

"Mara, this is Powell. Have you seen Afina?"

"Not since the restaurant."

"Did you see her outside after the shooting? Which direction she went?"

"No I didn't. I'm afraid I just ran for my life. Have you asked Emma and Becky?"

"They haven't seen her. I'm wondering if Victor has snatched her."

"I doubt it. Listen, I'm just about to jump in the shower. Can we talk later? I'll let you know if I hear from her," Mara promised.

"Thanks. You haven't heard anything further about Victor's whereabouts, I suppose?"

"Sorry, nothing."

Powell said thanks and ended the call.

"Who was that?" Victor asked suspiciously.

"A friend telling me Afina is missing."

"So we better get started." He handed the belt to Mara. "This bitch needs to be taught a proper lesson. She and Powell are responsible for Dimitry and Stefan being in jail."

"I'm not doing this," Mara said defiantly. "In fact, I'm leaving before the police arrive and if you have any bloody sense you will do the same."

"You're going nowhere," Victor said menacingly, taking a gun from his trouser belt. He pointed the weapon at Mara. "I saw you two together in that bar," he said distastefully. "I think you like this little bitch."

"Rubbish" Mara exclaimed. "I've just been doing what Stefan told me to do. Remember, you and her disappeared together. He told me to become her friend and keep an eye on her. Stefan thought she might be working for you."

"Working for me! Doing what exactly?"

"Going into competition."

"I've heard enough of this bollocks! Ever since this damned girl arrived in the country everything we do has turned to shit. This is your chance to prove she doesn't mean anything to you." He thrust the belt into Mara's hands.

Mara was torn between her feelings for Afina and her fear of Victor. She gripped the buckle in her hand and glanced at Afina. Despite her mouth being sealed, Afina's eyes were pleading with her to help. Mara moved to the bottom of the bed to avoid Afina's accusing look. If she tried to refuse to use the belt, Victor simply wasn't going to accept no for an answer. He would probably belt Afina twice as hard and may even decide Mara deserved a similar punishment.

"Damn," Mara swore, as she delivered a half-hearted blow with the belt.

"That was pathetic," Victor said.

Mara struck a little harder with the belt but she knew it was still well below Victor's expectations.

Victor grabbed the belt from Mara's hand and belted Afina with all his force. Her bottom desperately wriggled on the bed trying to avoid further blows.

"That is what I want to see. Do it properly or else..." Victor left the threat unfinished.

Mara realised she was stuck between the proverbial rock and a hard place. She had real feelings for Afina but if she didn't beat her with sufficient force then Victor was capable of getting really nasty.

If only the police or Powell would turn up. She needed to buy some time. "I need to take a piss," she said and started towards the door of the room. Victor quickly blocked her path. "I can't concentrate on doing this properly when I'm desperate for a pee."

"Don't be long," Victor warned.

Mara went straight to the bathroom, the very one which she knew Afina had originally used to escape. She could think of nothing which would deflect Victor from his intention to severely beat Afina. He was a sadist at heart and she had seen the pleasure he took from hurting many girls over the last couple of years. It was time for her to make a decision. If she left the bathroom and beat Afina as Victor wanted, then there would never be a chance for them to be friends in the future let alone lovers. She took her phone from her pocket and texted Powell.

"How long are you going to be in there," Victor shouted from outside.

"Just a minute," Mara replied after reading the immediate response from Powell. He was on his way but she knew it would take ten minutes from the Marina.

"Get out here now or I'll break the door down," Victor threatened.

Mara flushed the toilet and went to the sink. She turned the tap on and pretended to wash her hands for a minute. Then she opened the door to the bathroom.

"Let's get on with it," Victor demanded. He led the way back to the bedroom and picked up the belt from where Mara had left it on the bottom of the bed. "As you seem to lack strength, hold the belt like this and then hit her with the buckle. He demonstrated with a swing of his arm and this time Afina's whole body fought with the restraints to get free.

Mara observed the red trickle of blood where the point of the buckle had drawn a line across Afina's bottom. She took the belt from Victor and knew what she had to do. She walked to the other side of the bed as if about to start the beating. She laid the belt on the bed and quickly pulled her top over her head, revealing a lacy white bra.

"What the hell are you doing?" Victor asked.

"I'm getting comfortable," she replied, undoing her jeans and pulling them down her legs. I know from previous experience it's hot work beating someone and anyway don't you like it more this way?"

Victor seemed momentarily nonplussed and said nothing but looked appreciatively at her body. He smiled lasciviously. "You have a great body."

"Wouldn't you enjoy beating this body for the first time?"

"It has crossed my mind."

"Stefan's not around anymore and I've always wondered what it would be like receiving not giving… And you don't need to tie me down. I'll take it willingly from you. Wouldn't that make a nice change? I can bend over that chair and you can punish me for being a naughty girl."

Mara could sense the change in atmosphere in the room. Victor was now more focused on her than Afina. She threw the belt across the bed to Victor. "You can always deal with Afina once you've finished with me."

"You've been a very naughty girl," Victor agreed. "I shall have to teach you a lesson." He moved the chair to the side of the bed in such a position Afina could see everything. "Bend over," he instructed, indicating the chair.

Mara slowly removed her knickers and moved towards the chair but stopped in front of Victor with her eyes cast down to the ground. "I've been a very bad girl." She removed her bra directly in front of Victor. "I'm ready for my punishment. Unless you would like me to pleasure you first?"

"First you have the pain then you can have the pleasure."

Mara could think of nothing further she could do to buy time. She moved to the chair and leaned over the back. She wasn't quite tall enough and had to stand on her tip toes. She stretched her arms and held on to the seat of the chair. She had beaten dozens of girls over the previous couple of years but despite Victor asking more than once to beat her, she had always said no and fortunately Stefan had confirmed she was off limits. She waited for the first blow, praying he would not be using the buckle. She had quite happily indulged in some smacking in her private life but never been hit by any implement before.

"Make sure you count the strokes," Victor said. "You know the rules. Don't count properly and we start again."

Mara prepared herself and cast a glance to the side where she could see Afina, and forced a smile. When the first blow landed she was surprised that it wasn't quite as bad as she had expected. It hurt like hell but she was relieved to find he wasn't using the buckle. He delivered four more fast blows and suddenly the combination of the blows made it impossible for her not to squirm and move her bottom from side to side.

"Keep still," Victor ordered or we will begin again.

Mara took three more blows before she cried out, "Shit that hurts!"

That seemed to invigorate Victor and the next two blows were even harder. Mara knew she couldn't voluntarily take much more. She stood up and turned to face Victor. "I can't do it like this," she explained. "You need to tie me up like the others."

Victor seemed undecided for a second. "Okay," he agreed. "But for interrupting me we will start at the beginning again."

It must have been ten minutes. Where the hell is Powell? She was scared of the idea of being tied to the bed. It would give Victor carte blanche to beat her as much and as hard as he wanted.

Victor moved to the bed and undid Afina's leg ties. Then he withdrew the gun from his pocket and pointed it at Afina while he undid the wrist restraints.

"No messing, Afina. Just tie Mara to the bed, then go sit in the chair and watch the fun. It'll be your turn again soon enough."

CHAPTER FORTY EIGHT

Powell and two police cars full of armed officers arrived outside the house. Powell had convinced the officer in charge he needed to go along as he knew the layout of the house. A quick call to Chief Inspector Brown also confirmed he wasn't just your average civilian and could more than take care of himself. Powell explained who was in the house and a little of the background history.

They didn't announce their arrival with any sirens and as the seven officers joined him at the front door, Powell explained about the stairs leading to the different rooms and that the three people he knew to be in the house were in Stefan's rooms. That meant they had the disadvantage of having to scale three floors of stairs quietly to get to Victor, an almost impossible task.

"Listen Inspector, if you knock down the door and announce our arrival, Victor is likely to shoot the girls and some of us. I think I know him a little and neither do I think he will just come quietly."

"So what do you suggest we do?"

"I'll go in alone and try to contain Victor. I don't believe he will just shoot me so I should make it up to his room unharmed. We then need to coordinate that you take the door down and come up those stairs fast in say exactly ten minutes. Hopefully the diversion of your arrival will give me the opportunity to deal with Victor."

"I can't let you do that. We need to treat this as a kidnapping, contain the situation and start a negotiation with this Victor."

"Inspector, right now this dangerous lunatic is upstairs with Afina, who he wants dead. He has a sick mind and we don't have time to do it your way. He may well be slowly killing her right now so please let me get on and do what I do best."

Powell took out his wallet and retrieved a small tool he hadn't used for two years since he last locked himself out of his home. It took him less than a minute to open the front door while the Inspector watched with a disapproving face.

When the door eased open, Powell glanced at his watch. "I have nine thirty seven now. Cause the biggest disturbance possible at nine forty fifty. If you don't want to come up the stairs then turn on all your sirens and just make a shed load of noise."

"Okay, Powell. I'm sorry, I can't give you a weapon."

"That's all right, I don't need guns to take care of myself."

Powell turned and slowly entered the house, listening for sounds from above. He heard someone female scream and swear. He wasn't sure if it was Mara or Afina. He climbed the stairs swiftly on the balls of his feet, anxious to remain undetected for as long as possible. He guessed the scream had come from Afina's old bedroom and he made it to outside Stefan's lounge without detection. He turned the door handle and gently opened the door a few inches, half expecting to be challenged from inside but he could hear voices coming from Afina's room so he opened the door enough to see inside and found himself staring into an empty room.

Powell prayed his luck would continue as he took a few steps into the room. Victor was probably focused on whatever he was doing to Afina but Powell hated to contemplate what he was going to find once inside the room.

The internal door to Afina's bedroom was open and Powell could now hear clearly what was being said but as it was in Romanian he couldn't actually understand anything! Despite the language barrier, he could at least detect both Afina and Mara were still alive. Having safely made it this far, there was little point in waiting for the police to come charging up the stairs.

CHAPTER FORTY NINE

Freed of her bonds, Afina tore off the tape from around her mouth. "You're a sick bastard," she swore at Victor. Seeing what he had done to Mara and knowing he had only just started, she was now more angry than scared. Thanks to Powell, her family was safe and she had only to worry about herself. Actually, that wasn't true, she also had to worry about Mara, who had just selflessly convinced Victor to expend his anger on her body rather than Afina's.

"It's okay," Mara said. "I don't mind."

"Don't be stupid, Mara! Of course you fucking mind."

Victor waved his gun at both girls. "I would love to watch you two bitches arguing further but I don't have the time. "Afina, I suggest you tie Mara to the bed before I become impatient."

"Fuck you," Afina retorted. "I'm doing nothing to help your twisted games. Just shoot me if you want."

"Perhaps you have a good idea, Afina. Let's play a game. Tie Mara to the bed or I will shoot her."

Afina was surprised by Victor's suggestion. She was trying to protect Mara but now the only options were see her shot or see her beaten. She hesitated and Victor moved the gun menacingly towards Mara.

"This is your last chance, girls. I am going to count to ten and Mara had better be tied to the bed or she will learn what it is like to be shot in the knee. Believe me, it is agony. One, Two…" Victor counted slowly.

Mara lay down on the bed. "Tie me up, Afina. I don't want to lose my knee."

Victor said, "Three."

Afina felt she had no damn choice and started to move toward the bed to do as instructed.

The calm was shattered by Powell hurtling through the door and throwing himself in a rugby like tackle at Victor's body, knocking him off balance and sending him crashing to the floor.

Mara shot up from the bed and Afina stepped backwards in shock as the two men wrestled on the floor.

Victor still had the gun in his hand and used it as a club on the side of Powell's head. There wasn't much room for the two men as they were squashed between the bed, chair and furniture.

"Get out," Powell screamed.

Afina was trapped in the corner, unable to get past the two men. She witnessed Victor again strike Powell's head with the gun. She looked around for some form of weapon so she could help Powell.

Victor's blows with the gun had achieved the desired effect and a dazed Powell was unable to resist Victor pushing him off his body. As Victor climbed unsteadily to his feet, he aimed the gun at Powell and Afina knew she had to do something. She picked up the chair and brought it down on Victor's back. The impact had little effect.

Victor turned towards her, surprised by the new assault. He pointed the gun at her and Afina knew he was going to pull the trigger and this time there could be no escape.

Mara was now standing and when she saw Victor's intent screamed, "Noooo," at the top of her voice.

Victor turned towards Mara as she threw herself at him. He fired and the noise in the confined bedroom space was magnified to a terrible extent.

Afina saw the limp body of Mara fall against Victor and knock him to the ground. In the confined space, he struggled for a few seconds to push her away.

Powell had recovered some strength and climbed unsteadily to his feet just as Victor managed to push Mara aside. Powell saw Victor raise his gun and take aim but before he could fire, Powell threw himself forwards, using both his hands to pin Victor's gun hand to the floor.

They rolled on the floor for a few seconds, neither able to gain the upper hand. Victor tried a head-butt but Powell was able to avoid it at the last moment.

Powell could see Victor's exposed throat and releasing his right hand from the arm wrestling match with Victor's gun hand, reverted to his basic MI5 training and chopped at the throat. The effect was immediate and Victor was desperately struggling to breathe. He dropped the gun and his hands instinctively went up to his throat, to the source of his pain.

Powell took the opportunity to grab Victor around his neck in an arm lock. He wrapped his legs around Victor's body for greater leverage. Victor responded by desperately trying to claw at Powell's arms and face as the grip tightened, slowly squeezing the life out of Victor.

There was the sudden sound of men rushing up the stairs shouting, "Police. Throw down your weapons and get on the floor."

Powell kept hold of Victor's throat, even when the police burst into the room. There had been no further resistance from Victor but he wasn't going to repeat his error of letting him live, to come back seeking further revenge.

Afina could finally get to Mara. "She's been shot, call an ambulance," she shouted but deep inside she suspected it was already too late.

CHAPTER FIFTY

Twenty four hours had passed since the rescue of Afina and Powell had spent many of them at the hospital. Mara was on a life support system and her chances were less than fifty per cent.

Afina hadn't left the room since arriving and was keeping vigil on Mara, refusing all suggestions she should go home and rest. Mara was in bed with tubes in her arms and hooked up to machines monitoring her heart beat and breathing. She looked surprisingly peaceful given the traumatic nature of a gunshot wound.

By the time the police had forced Powell to let go of Victor he was indeed certified as dead. Powell had zero regrets about his actions and Afina's testimony combined with Mara's being shot, was sufficient to exonerate him of any charge of using excessive force. Powell realised he had not changed as much as he had thought over the last twenty years because he had ended Victor's life without a minute's troubled thought, either at the time or since. It was further evidence that he was ready to return to a different line of work.

Powell even had a tinge of regret he had allowed Dimitry to live but at least he was going to spend the rest of his life in prison. Bella's death had introduced him to a world he barely knew existed and he was determined to dedicate the remainder of his life to more than propping up a bar. He had spoken with Brian and his support was going to prove useful although it would naturally have to be unofficial. Brian even had a couple of potential projects, which sounded interesting but first Powell knew he must help Afina through the next few days, before he moved on to helping others in need of his services.

Afina had been quiet and withdrawn since Mara's shooting and though she had expressed her gratitude to Powell, he was sure she was feeling terribly guilty. He tried to make her see it was purely Victor's fault but she wasn't really listening. He was going to encourage her to go home to Bucharest for a while, if not permanently, once Mara's situation was resolved.

Powell walked to the coffee machine for the hundredth time and fetched two more terrible tasting drinks simply labelled as white coffee. His mobile rang and glancing at the caller, he saw it was Brian so decided to ignore the warning signs saying use of mobiles was forbidden, within the hospital.

"Hello, Brian. What's up?"

"How is Mara doing?"

"Not great, she's still in a coma but she has a fighting chance. Problem is the doctors have no idea if or when she might come out of the coma."

"Sorry to hear that. I know it's probably bad timing but I'm going to send you a file I'd like you to take a look at. I think it's something you might be interested in."

"Give me the brief story."

"A woman with friends in high places married a Saudi citizen and they settled over here. Two children later he decides he's no longer in love with her and has gone back home."

"What do you need me for?"

"He's taken the children with him and not allowing the mother any access. Everything possible has been done through official channels but unless someone helps her get her kids out of Saudi, she may never see them again."

"Okay, I'll read the file and speak to you soon."

CHAPTER FIFTY ONE

The phone rang but Powell didn't recognise the number.

"Powell," he answered.

A male voice said, "Hello Mr. Powell, this is Doctor Roberts from Sussex Hospital. You are listed as next of kin for Mara Petrescu. Is that correct?"

Powell took in a deep breath. "That is correct. Do you have some news?" he asked anxiously.

"Yes Mr Powell, I have some good news. Miss Petrescu has awoken from her coma. She is very weak and it's still early days but there is every reason to be positive."

Powell was relieved and excited by the news. "Thank you, doctor. You've made my day."

"Actually, that's why I like to make these type of calls in person. I spend too much time delivering bad news."

"She's been in the coma for ten days, will there be any lasting effect?"

"There shouldn't be but sometimes complications do arise."

"Is she speaking?" He had found fifty thousand pounds in his bank account and he was pretty sure it must have been Mara who returned the money he had paid to Stefan. He was desperate for her to wake from the coma so he could say thanks.

"A little but she still needs to rest and recuperate so don't expect any long conversations at first. I have to go now but feel free to have a brief visit as soon as is convenient."

"Thanks again, doctor. You really have made my day." As Powell ended the call he felt like a huge weight had been lifted from his shoulders.

His phone rang again before he could tell Afina the good news.

"Hello Brian. I guess you're chasing me for an answer about the Bennett woman but first I have some good news. I just heard from the hospital and Mara is out of her coma. The doctor thinks she should make a full recovery."

There was a pause at the other end of the phone before Brian spoke, "That is really good news but I'm afraid I'm the bearer of some not so good news. Dimitry has escaped. He was in court today to be charged with additional crimes and a couple of armed men helped him get away."

"How the hell could that happen?" Powell asked angrily.

"They were professionals, Powell. They had automatic weapons, killed three people and injured several others. They knew what they were doing."

Powell could barely believe what he was hearing. "Sorry, I know it's not your fault. An escape like that takes a load of planning. How has that been possible with him locked up? Someone must have liaised between Dimitry and the men on the outside."

"We're looking closely at everyone who has contact with him but the likely source is the solicitor. He's Romanian, been living in England for only a few months and not known to have been involved with any other high profile cases. He might be bent or they might simply have leaned on his family."

"I wonder if Dimitry knows Powell and Danny are the same man?"

"There's no real way of telling unless he turns up on your doorstep."

"I can't imagine he'll come anywhere near Brighton but I'll be careful. Anyway, I need to get on with the Bennett case so I expect to be travelling a great deal."

"So you will help her?"

"I've done a bit of background research. The next step is to meet her before I make a final decision."

"I'll check when she's available in the next few days and get back to you with some suggestions. She will be over the moon to hear you want to help, she's really desperate."

"I want to help but I haven't made a final decision because I don't want to go saying I will get her children back for her and then fail. That would be like torturing her further. I have to believe I can succeed before I take the job."

"I understand. Listen, I'm sorry about the Dimitry news. Make sure Afina is safe."

"Of course," Powell replied a little tetchy. He didn't need reminding to take care of Afina.

"There's a massive manhunt taking place. As you can imagine, the boys in blue are feeling pretty sick he escaped and he'll do well to evade capture for long."

"Based on the organisation needed to break him out of the courtroom, I think we can safely assume he would also have had a plan for what happened once he was free, so I wouldn't be confident the police will catch him. Anyway, thanks for letting me know, Brian. I need to get back to Afina."

"Stay alert," Brian warned. "You seem like a magnet for trouble recently."

Powell ended the call. As he walked upstairs to Afina's apartment, he was hoping Dimitry would stay away from Brighton but if he did turn up, he would hopefully still believe Danny was a friend. That would be ironic and almost comical.

"I have some very good news and some bad news," Powell said, when Afina invited him in. "Which do you want to hear first?"

CHAPTER FIFTY TWO

Afina's mother had enjoyed the three weeks of having no one else to cook or clean for but she had missed the girls and the apartment seemed very empty and quiet. She had always known the day would arrive when her girls would leave home but she had been caught by surprise with the suddenness with which it had happened.

She was looking forward to seeing Adriana, who was on her way back from the airport and was due back at school in two days. There were only two weeks of term left until the summer holidays and they had spoken about the possibility of her then spending some more time in England. For at least the next two weeks life would return to something like normal.

She suspected Afina would be in England for a long time to come but that wasn't a bad thing. She was confident Powell would look after Afina. He was a good man even if his eyes showed him to be a sad man. She wasn't going to be surprised if one day in the future, Afina announced she and Powell were living together properly. There was a definite attraction between the two of them. She wasn't sure how she felt about her daughter going out with someone older than she was. Still, there was no point telling Afina what to do as she would always choose her own path.

The knock at the door led to her rushing to the door in expectation of welcoming Adriana back home. For the first time in two weeks she didn't bother putting the chain on the door before opening it to see who was outside. It probably would have made little difference because as soon as the door was ajar, a heavy boot kicked the door inwards, knocking her flying backwards as the door crashed into her body.

She was stunned by the impact of the door and lying on the hallway floor as two sets of arms grabbed her by each arm and dragged her along the ground into the living room. A chair was taken from the kitchen into the lounge and nothing was said, as her arms were tied behind the back of the chair.

She was feeling dazed and had a large swelling on her forehead. She slowly focused her mind on what was happening but decided to keep her eyes closed. She felt tape being wrapped around her mouth.

"Damn door hit her in the head, she's barely conscious," Bogdan said.

Dimitry took her chin in his hand and shook it from side to side. "Wake up woman, we need to talk to you."

She stirred and slowly opened her eyes. She felt like asking who the fuck they were but the tape made it impossible and anyway, she knew in her heart who they were and why they were there. Afina had called and told her just a few days earlier that Dimitry had escaped from the English prison and would probably try to return to Bucharest.

"We want to find Afina," Dimitry said. "You are going to tell us where to find her."

She felt fear in her heart but not for herself, not even for Afina, who had Powell to help but for Adriana, who was due home very shortly. She prayed they would be gone before Adriana arrived.

"Get me a glass of water," Dimitry instructed Bogdan. "I'm going to remove the tape. Don't make any noise or I will hurt you." He ripped the tape from her mouth.

Bogdan returned with a glass of water, handed it to Dimitry and he in turn held it to her lips. She drank a little.

"So where is Afina?" Dimitry asked.

"She is in England."

"I know she is in England but where is she?"

"She is in Brighton."

"I fucking know she's in Brighton but where is she?" Dimitry shouted impatiently.

"I'm not sure. She calls me sometimes but I don't know where she is living."

"That's a pity. It would save you a great deal of pain if you could just tell me something, which would help me find Afina."

"I know she moved from where she was originally staying but I don't have any other details."

Without warning Dimitry wrapped more tape around her mouth. "Let's take her to the bedroom," he said.

They untied her and supporting each arm half carried, half dragged her to the bedroom.

"Hold her up." Dimitry said. He roughly tore and pulled off her clothes until she was naked. "Did you know I had the pleasure of fucking Afina the day she arrived in England? No, I guess she wouldn't share those sort of details with her mother. She has a nice body but a very tight arse. I have a very large cock as you will discover in the minute and it was difficult getting all of it into Afina's tight little arse but we managed it in the end. Now we will discover if you are equally as tight."

She heard the front door opening and knew it could only be one person.

"Hello mama," Ariana called out. "I am home."

She had been pretending to be weaker than she felt. She summoned up all her strength and kicked out at Dimitry's crotch.

"Bitch," he shouted, bent double and in serious pain.

In the same instant she threw her head backwards and connected with Bogdan's nose. He released his grip on her arms and she tore the tape from her mouth.

"Run Adriana," she screamed at the top of her voice. "Get help."

Dimitry punched her in the face and she collapsed to the floor.

Afina found Powell downstairs in the bar.

"Did Adriana get home okay?" Powell asked and then seeing the tears streaming down her face asked, "What's wrong?"

"Dimitry went to my mother's apartment. There were two of them and God knows what they would have done to my mother but Adriana came home and she ran for help."

"Are they both okay?" Powell asked, deeply concerned.

"My mother has a fractured jaw but otherwise she is okay. They didn't touch Adriana. She was lucky, as she ran out on to the street to look for help, two policemen came to her assistance. When they went upstairs there was no sign of Dimitry. He had probably taken the fire escape. What are we going to do, Powell? With Dimitry free my family can never be safe."

Powell had to agree that it was impossible for Afina to move on with her life while Dimitry was at large. To his mind this latest attack by Dimitry was the straw that finally broke the camel's back. Powell had encountered similar people before, who only knew how to use violence and terror to achieve their criminal aims. Like Dimitry, they were usually arrogant and felt themselves superior to those around them, not recognising the limits others lived their lives by. Well Powell had reached his limits of restraint. Bella would understand it was imperative he acted promptly to cut out the cancer that was putting so many people's lives in danger. There was no other option.

"I will deal with Dimitry," Powell said with conviction. "Where are your mother and Adriana staying?"

"Mama is in hospital and Adriana is staying with a friend. What are you going to do?"

"I'm going to visit Bucharest again and I promise you I won't come home until Dimitry is no longer a danger to your family. There's something you should know though before I go. If anything happens to me, I have changed my will so you will inherit the bar."

"What do you mean, I inherit the bar?"

"You will own the bar." He didn't bother to add, as sole beneficiary she would also own his house and everything else. "But don't get too excited, I fully intend to live for a very long time."

Afina couldn't stop her tears. She ran into Powell's arms and gave him a huge hug. "You are too kind."

"I know it's what Bella would have wanted. You and she would have liked each other."

"It is too dangerous for you to go to Bucharest, Powell. I don't want you killed as well."

"I can look after myself and remember, despite what Dimitry has done to you and your family, I have a more powerful reason than any of you for wanting to see him behind bars."

THE END

Read Bill Ward's thriller ABDUCTION.

Powell returns in an action packed novel of violence, sex and betrayal!

He is trying to recover two children from Saudi Arabia, who have been abducted by their father. In a culture where women are second class citizens, a woman holds the key to the success or failure of his mission.

Meanwhile, back in Brighton, Afina is trying to deal with a new threat from Romanian gangsters.

From the streets of Brighton to Riyadh, Powell must take the law into his own hands, to help the innocent.

Read Bill Ward's thriller REVENGE.

There is no greater motivator for evil than a huge sense of injustice!

Tom Ashdown, an unlikely hero, owns a betting shop in Brighton and gambles with his life when he stumbles across an attempted kidnapping, which leaves him entangled in a dangerous chain of events involving the IRA, a sister seeking revenge for the death of her brother and an informer in MI5 with a secret in his past.

Revenge is a fast paced thriller, with twists and turns at every step.

In a thrilling and violent climax everyone is intent on some form of revenge.

5* Reviews

"Revenge is an example of everything that I look for in an action thriller that involves suspense, betrayal and of course the key element revenge."

"A quality piece of work by an assured hand."

"This action packed thriller reads like a blockbuster movie!"

"Interesting characters and a compelling plot!"

"Move over Peter James, you have a serious rival!"

Read Bill Ward's thriller ENCRYPTION.

In a small software engineering company in England, a game changing algorithm for encrypting data has been invented, which will have far reaching consequences for the fight against terrorism.

The Security Services of the UK, USA and China all want to control the new software.

The Financial Director has been murdered and his widow turns to her brother-in-law to help discover the truth. But he soon finds himself framed for his brother's murder.

When the full force of government is brought to bear on one family, they seem to face impossible odds. Is it an abuse of power or does the end justify the means?

Only one man can find the answers but he is being hunted by the same people he once called friends and colleagues.

5* Reviews

"A Great English Spy Thriller."

"This is a great story! Once I started reading it, I could not put it down."

"A superior read in a crowded genre!"

"Full of memorable characters and enough twists and turns to impress all diehard thriller junkies, it is a wonderful read"

"If you're a fan of Ludlum, and love descriptive prose like that of Michener, you'll be right at home."

ABOUT THE AUTHOR

Bill Ward lives in Brighton with his German partner Anja. He has recently retired from senior corporate roles in large IT companies and is now following a lifelong passion for writing! With 7 daughters, a son, stepson, 2 horses, a dog, 2 cats, and 2 guinea pigs, life is always busy!

Bill's other great passion is following West Brom who he has been supporting for over fifty years.

Buy all Bill's books at leading online stores including:
amazon.com/Bill-Ward/e/B00F154DZ2/re
amazon.co.uk/Bill-Ward/e/B00F154DZ2/re

Connect with Bill online:

Twitter: http://twitter.com/billward10bill

Facebook: http://facebook.com/billwardbooks

Printed in Great Britain
by Amazon